DESCEND: HINTON CHARTER

BOOK 1

LEE DAWNA

LEEDAWNA BOOKS

First edition

Cover design by Premade Ebook Cover Shop

www.premadeebookcovershop.com

ISBN 978-1-949192-07-0 (paperback)

ISBN 978-1-949192-06-3 (ebook)

Published by LeeDawna Books www.leedawnabooks.com

leedawnabooks@suddenlink.net

This book is dedicated to my son. You are forever my hero.

~1~

The great thing about living in a small town is the exact same thing that makes living in a place like Hinton terrible. Everybody knows everybody. If *knowing* means gossiping about all the bad things a person has done in their life; as if that one day, or sometimes one minute, defines the entirety of who a person is. Like Tommy Pillsbory jumping off the roof of his garage when he was eight, thinking he could fly like Superman with that old bedsheet tied around his neck. He managed to nearly hang himself from the bucket of his grandpa's John Deere.

Tommy is a dentist now, and I'd swear the tab he runs up in my cousin's bar every night is because even his wife still pretends he's as dumb as the rock his buddy Warren launched through old lady Gideon's kitchen window. In Warren's defense, I was on a balcony above that window, littering their heads with the baby snakes I dug out of the backyard. Needless to say, none of us got a slice of the old lady's rhubarb pie that day.

Then there's that time Layla Alderidge peed her pants in third grade. The girl had social anxiety like a tornado on steroids, but all anyone ever paid attention to was how *weird* she was. Meaning she wasn't loud and obnoxious like the rest of us. She kept to herself and just stared at you when you talked to her, a personality she never grew out of. She did lose the lanky limbs and grow into her nose, though. Once puberty hit, she was as stunning as the sun rising over the river at dawn. Last anyone around here heard of her was the talk of the similarities between the body found thrown over the side of the only highway out of this county and the tattoos a teenage Layla was rumored to have in places only the men in town could attest to.

As for me, I'm not above tossing a snake if the occasion calls for it, and if Warren gets anywhere near me again, it'll be calling. Other than that, despite my reputation for being two shades shy of a crayon box, I'm an accountant. Now, don't ask anyone around here to do that math because they'll just tell you how I keep the books for my cousin's bar, and how he's a member of the notorious outlaw biker club the Leidolf—Descendants of the Wolf. Those two things are true. I even sometimes moonlight as a bartender. But that's only because cousin Gary lets me use the office just behind the bar as my own, and he started opening the building at nine every morning, adding a full kitchen to serve meals and everything, so I could use his charter's clubhouse to meet with my other clients instead of me having to rent an office or work from home where people would feel free to stop by my house whenever they felt like it.

While Gary does favor me, he didn't *only* expand the bar into daytime use for my benefit. He knew doing so would go a long way in making the Leidolf less scary to the townspeople. Admittedly, no one was happy when my long-lost cousin rolled back into town wearing a kutte and heading up a row of bikers donning the same leather battle jackets. But Gary was born and raised on the banks of the New River, and like the rest of us, this mud is in his veins.

It didn't take long for the twenty-six members of his new family to get it stuck in theirs either. Five years ago they made living here official, Gary heading up this new Hinton charter of the Leidolf. They bought and renovated an old building on the corner of Pleasant and Stokes, where the river whitecaps beyond the members-only parking lot out back and the rhododendron grow thick on the embankment, wrapping around the side of the building open to Stokes Street to provide natural fencing for the property.

Being fifteen years my senior, Gary was long gone by the time I entered high school. He'd call me nearly every day, though, on the phone he gave a six-year-old me before he left. I hid, cherished, and protected that phone because in a lot of ways, Gary was more like a dad to me than a cousin. "Tessa," he'd say, "are you okay? Is everyone treating you right?" I'd always tell him they were, not confiding in him the way I should have because I knew deep down that if I did, Gary would kill my father. Because another thing that's special about a small town is its secrets. No one has them. *Everyone* has them.

Evildoers hide their deeds. The victims hide their pain. Sometimes we mutate our pain into shame, knowing that if we tell what someone did to us, people will look at us as if *we're* to blame. In the end, all of our actions, whether it be the things we do or the ones we don't, it all comes down to fear. In eighth grade, my art teacher had a heart attack and was out of school for the last three months of the year. The substitute, Ms. Shinnston, hung a quote on the wall of our room. It was from some guy named Edmund Burke. I never bothered to see who he was, but I did read that quote every day, understanding the words on a visceral level. *"No passion so effectually robs the mind of all its powers of acting and reasoning as fear."*

I'd known from an early age that survival meant two things. Staying away from the bad guys, and if you couldn't get away, being willing to fight hard enough to let them know that they'd have to kill you to make you stop fighting. I was four the first and last time my dad physically abused me. I'd seen him beat, rape and torture my mom enough times to know he was bad, but it wasn't until he came after me that I learned to fight like a wildcat. My sister Beth never learned that skill. Nor did any of the other women, children, and weak men I watched Dad manipulate and torture over the years. Most of them are in my family, and their minds have been robbed of reason, their willpower sapped. All that powers them is fear. When Gary left, trading our lineage for the brotherhood of the Leidolf, he traded up. And that's saying something considering the club gained their reputation on rumors of being killers for hire.

None of the Leidolf have ever been locked up for murder. But whether they've killed or not, it's as sure as rain that they aren't cowards who hide behind women and children. The descendants have lines I know not to cross, and it's a shame that pedophiles and rapists who are either let out of jail or never sentenced to begin with don't know about those lines, but in the midst of the Leidolf den, I've never feared for my own safety—or that of any other female coming and going from Riverside Grille.

On many occasions, I've stayed in one of the apartments above the Grille, sleeping up there just as soundly as ever whether it be in Gary's apartment, his right-hand man Chopper's, or either of the other two that are open to any members of the club who want to crash here. I do have a house, a little place I bought on my own that I plan to fix up, but I let Beth move in with me and though I love my sister, she drains me. With Beth, there is *always* drama because she creates it. She lies, lies about lying, and pulls off indignant rage better than a Hollywood actress. I'd rather be at the bar. Even Chief Dunbar and his men frequent the Grille. And we don't talk about the many occasions when we find local clergy *counseling* some poor woman in a dark booth. I mean, this *is* the Bible Belt. We've got a lot of lost souls in need of saving.

"Howdie, Chief." I place a cold mug on the bar as he strolls toward me. "The usual?"

He looks over my shoulder, down the hall past where my office is. The heart of the club is there, the doors beside my office leading to the inner sanctum, the *church*, a long-walled room I've never been inside. All I know is my office is carved from a piece of it, the two walls of the office bordering the room reinforced with steel and noise-canceling foam. Across the hall from the church is Gary's office, and next to that the stairs leading to the apartments above. At the end of the hall is a solid metal door that leads to the back parking lot, our members-only access that also extends to staff who aren't part of the club, people like me who are close friends.

Hooking his thumbs through his belt, still wearing his uniform, Chief glances around the bar, noting the location of each and every club member. "Where's Gary?"

I cock my head. "Upstairs. Why?"

He eyes Chopper, who is sitting in his usual spot at the end of the bar. Chopper doesn't talk much, he barely makes eye contact with anyone, but it's no secret he's the club member feared most. Chief jerks a chin in Chopper's direction. "He been here all day?"

"Yep," I lie. I've been in my office and have no idea. "All of them have been here all day, so whatever you're trying to frame my boys for, they have an alibi."

His teeth clench. "I already know he hasn't been here so cut the crap, this is serious."

I lean on the bar. "I went with Chopper and Gary on a store run this afternoon, but we're not thieves, we paid our bill. So I hope this isn't you coming in here trying to frame me in order to collect some *other* form of payment."

"Darn it, Tessa!" He slams a palm on the counter, gaining the attention of every wolf in the bar tonight. "A body washed up on the riverbank this morning."

I jolt upright. "Who?"

He leans toward me, voice low, and snarled. "Samantha. Gary's girlfriend. She was gutted like a fish. So you go get me Gary right now."

~2~

Numb, I traverse the stairs, Chopper coming up behind me after having escorted Chief into the back lot. "This is going to devastate Gary," I whisper.

Chopper moves ahead of me, one solid rap of knuckles against Gary's door. It swings open. Gary's skin is pale. Eyes rimmed in red. His hand shakes as he lowers the phone from his ear. Someone delivered the news already. "Samantha." He mutters her name.

I nod. "Chief is out back."

He walks into the hall, Chopper steadying him when he wobbles. Gary reaches for my hand. I grip his, walking with him down the stairs and out the back door. We meet Chief at the corner of the building. "What happened?" Gary asks, voice stronger than I know he feels.

Chief sighs. "That's what I'm here to find out. Where were you this morning?"

"Here," Gary answers. "Samantha was here, too. Until about seven."

"What happened at seven?" Chief asks.

Gary's eyes narrow. "She left. Got in her car and drove away. And no, she's not back on drugs. So I'm going to ask again, what happened to Samantha?"

Chief wipes his mouth. "It's bad." None of us say a word. Chief's throat bobs. "Do you remember that body getting pulled out of the river four years ago? The one with the missing head and hands?" We nod and he swallows again. "Well, Samantha's head and hands are still attached, but other parts of her are missing."

The atmosphere changes, a crack of thunder exploding from Gary's chest. Felt. Almost heard. But not seen. Chief stares at him and takes a shaky breath. Gary's known to be a kind man. A fair man. But he isn't someone you want to cross, and Chief understands that. He runs a hand around to the back of his neck. "I shouldn't be telling you this, and I expect you to keep it quiet, but Samantha's heart is missing. And I know that because she's cut wide open, chin to shin, if you understand what I'm saying."

I turn aside, puking up everything I've eaten for a month. I never could handle the sight of blood, and apparently I can't handle hearing about it either. Chopper grabs my elbow, steadying me and being my pillar of strength.

Gary clutches his chest. "Missing?"

Chief nods, providing more imagery that I don't need. "Cut out. Gone. She's fileted open like a science experiment." He reigns himself in, the weight of what he's seen a tug at the seams of his façade. He glances at Chopper's hand on my arm, the tight way his fingers have me pulled against his side. "We'll know more once we get the coroner's report."

Gary's legs give and his six-foot frame drops to the asphalt. I kneel beside him and Chopper boxes Chief out while tears soak Gary's face. He tucks his head in his hands. "I was just with her."

For the people he loves, my cousin has the most tender heart you'll find. And he loved Samantha, though their relationship was complicated. She was an addict and when she was using, he wouldn't allow her in the bar. He'd watch after her, get her help, take her to her mom's trailer and stay there with her, the two of them fighting to keep Samantha clean when she was too weak to fight for herself. When the intervention took and she got clean, their relationship was beautiful. When she fell off into the abyss of prescription pills, being her rock depleted him.

Chief clears his throat. "I need to get your statement, Gary. Official and on the record."

Chopper nods at Rick and Zeno, our unofficial back door guards. The club has no rivals or threats in this usually slow-moving riverside town. Hinton is nestled between the mountains and the river, the railroad and a handful of well-kept homes from bygone days the only reminders of the prosperity that once flooded this place—wealth pulled out of the mountains in the form of coal. Still, a couple of club members can always be found hanging around in this back lot.

Without a word, Chief begins to move down the alleyway toward the front of the building as the men approach him. "Have him wait for me," I tell Zeno. He nods.

Helping Chopper get Gary onto his feet, I go inside with them and pull back the sheets of Gary's bed just before Chopper settles him into it. I tuck Gary in while Chopper grabs a bottle of McDowell's from the liquor cabinet Gary keeps stocked in his kitchen.

Pouring Gary a shot, Chopper hands it to him. Gary slams it and motions for another. Chopper obliges. I place a hand on his shoulder. "I'll be back in a few minutes."

I leave the room, knowing Chopper will stay by Gary's side. I run down the stairs and exit the back door, turning the corner and walking up the alley beyond where the rhododendrons grow. Chief is just ahead, shoulder leaned against the wall as he stares at his phone. I move in close to him. "Gary isn't going to be fit to talk for a while. I can fill you in on his movements. If there's something I don't know, I'll ask him when he's up to it and text you."

His head shakes. "I can't have a paper trail of us talking. Don't text me until I get this cleared."

"We have cases of burner phones, Chief."

He presses the heel of his hand into his eye, the way you do when a migraine is kicking up. "Fine, text me. But I'm still going to need an official interview with Gary. He needs to come down to the station first thing in the morning."

"He's not going to be up for that."

"A girl is dead!" he growls. "I don't care how he *feels*, Samantha is dead and I need answers."

I lean forward. "So does Gary."

His lips peel away from his teeth. "He just confessed to being with her last night *and* this morning. It doesn't look like her body was in the water long before Duncan found her. At ten o'clock. Those facts don't look good for Gary."

I press my own shoulder to the wall, finding I need the strength of the old cinderblock to reinforce me. "Duncan found her?"

Chief puts his phone away. "Yeah, he was fishing this morning and…hooked her through the exposed ribcage. Blind old fool thought he had a real nice one."

Bile rises foamy in the back of my throat. "Where was she?"

"Floating against the bank in that swimmin' hole all you kids climb over the bank to go to."

He looks as ill as I feel. I wrap my arms around him. I don't like his lack of morals but I'm not his wife, so cheating spouse or not, this man saw something I'm having a hard time just hearing about.

Slowly, Chief brings his hands up to pat my back, rests them there, both giving and taking a real hug, and then he pries us apart. "I *need* that interview with Gary. And I can't do it here. It's got to be official because…"

"Surely you don't think Gary is capable of killing his own girlfriend."

His jaw ticks. "I *know* he's capable of killing. But no, I don't think he'd… Listen, me taking him in with handcuffs is going to turn every busybody in town into a prosecutor. I don't want to do him that way. But there are things at play here that are far outside of my control. Gary *has* to come to the station first thing, promise me you'll have him there."

I fold my arms. "I'll promise you no such thing. *If* Gary's capable of leaving the bar tomorrow, it'll only be to do *your* job. He'll find out who killed his woman."

His teeth clench, words coming out in a hiss. "Gary's DNA was on Layla."

The numbness from earlier returns, starting in my legs and quaking upward. I give the wall more of my weight. "His what was where?"

Chief thrusts a hand through his sandy-gray hair. "His DNA, it was…there was a t-shirt near that mutilated body four years ago. Gary's, I suppose. He never identified it and the body was out of my jurisdiction so it wasn't my case, but I did review the file. His DNA was on the shirt. So was Layla's blood. I talked to the detective and he said Gary put up an alibi and the prosecutor never thought there was enough to bring charges." His eyes meet mine. "We all know how y'all work alibis, and even if Gary admitted the t-shirt was his, he'd say he lost it at the laundromat."

"You're sure the body was Layla's then?"

He swallows. "Positive."

I plow the toe of my boot into his shin. "You're disgusting."

He jumps back, nursing his leg. "I never laid a finger on that child, and you know good and well I would *never* hurt a kid like that. She had a birthmark on her upper thigh. One of her tattoos was made to blend with it, but when you looked closely, it was still visible. I drove over to Mount Hope and had her folks take a look. They said it was her and gave a DNA sample to confirm."

"Why didn't you tell us?"

He shrugs. "The case is still open but long cold, not enough manpower to work it. Especially when her folks don't care enough to make any noise. According to them, when they moved out of town, she didn't move with them. Said she found a place to stay and was going to finish high school. They never heard from her again and never heard about the body or the rumors. I was the first law person they spoke to."

"Sounds like some top-notch detective work."

He tucks his thumbs back into his belt. "Yeah, well, Samantha *was* killed in my town, thrown in *my* river, where *my* kids swim. I'm going to find who did this to her."

I look across the alley to where Matt is standing in the window of his insurance office, watching us. Usually I flirt with him mercilessly because he's shy but hotter than a firecracker on the Fourth of July. Today, I can't even muster the strength to wave back at him. "Chief, if we both know Gary didn't do this to Layla or Samantha, then who did?"

He moves in front of me, blotting out my view of Matt. "Someone close enough to plant one of Gary's t-shirts with a dead girl, and close enough to know when Gary's DNA will be all over another. I asked you where Chopper was today for a reason."

~3~

My heart pounds against its cage as Chief lays out his theory for me. He thinks Chopper, who has been Gary's shadow since the day Gary came back to town, is secretly in love with Gary and killing off women who are a threat to his romantic pursuit. It's true that Layla grew into a beautiful girl, that drop-dead gorgeous that turns women green with envy and men into slobbering fools. Even the older ones. The ones who shouldn't be touching young girls. It's also true that in the beginning, when I first met Chopper, I too wondered if his love for Gary was of the romantic nature. Since then, I've learned that it isn't.

What Gary and Chopper share is a bond of absolute trust. Of absolute acceptance. They have a meeting of the minds, and that kind of connection works well for a man who prefers not to speak. Chopper can convey his thoughts to Gary with a look, and if there's something to be said, he lets Gary say it. And all the women Chief thinks are creeped out by Chopper's stringy hair, wiry muscles, and overly quiet nature are putty when Chopper sets his smoky eyes on them. So much so that I've teased Chopper about only keeping his head down as much as he does as a means of preventing the female folk from jumping him. Each time, he rightly tells me that they jump him even when his eyes don't summon them. I know I did.

"If Chopper's ever killed anyone, it would have been a terrible person and Samantha wasn't terrible. Misguided when it came to drugs, but she had a good soul, Chief. That's why Gary loved her."

"Gary loving her is my point," Chief clarifies.

I shake my head. "People have treated Gary like a bad egg ever since that rope swing broke and he crashed into the river's rocks instead of the water. He never grew out of the scar and around here, a facial scar automatically means a bad reputation. Though you don't want to cross him on a bad day, deep down he's softer than a newborn kitten. Chopper's not quite as soft, he's more like a wire-haired grizzly. But one who *only* eats vipers. Male ones at that. They don't hurt women."

He rubs his eyes. "To hear you tell it, the Leidolf are all upstanding citizens. But after they came to town, someone murdered two girls. And it wasn't the tooth fairy."

I lift a brow. "So because you've ruled out mythical creatures, it has to be a member of the club?"

He glares at me. I shrug. "Chief, we all want the same thing. Justice for Layla and Samantha. And you wouldn't be standing here talking to me if you really thought Gary *or* Chopper had something to do with the murders. And what makes you think the same person killed them both anyway? Layla was found years ago. And don't people usually kill in the same way?"

His jaw works. "It's just a gut feeling I have."

I roll my eyes. "And now we're back to feelings and mythical creatures."

His fingers circle my wrist, digging in. "There are three others."

I tug but he doesn't let go. "Three other what?"

He leans close to my ear. "Bodies. Now you go console your cousin and get me that meeting because we're getting ready to have a tidal wave of fear sweep this town and I will *not* let people panic. Do you understand me?"

My head shakes, not wanting to hear any more while my mouth asks without consent, "Who?"

He lets go of my wrist but stays close, glancing down the alley to where Zeno is watching us. "You can't repeat any of this. I haven't even told my officers yet but I'm going to have to soon." His eyes snap to mine, mouth too close to my own. "The others didn't die today, and they didn't die here. There's been a body found in every county bordering ours every year since Layla." He lets that sink in. "I heard about one of the cases and started digging. Before today, I was pretty certain it was the same killer. Now I'm convinced of it. They're evolving. Or devolving. I'm not sure which way to look at it, but the bodies are always mutilated in some way, and I know in my gut these women were all killed by the same person. And that person either lives in my town or decided to pay us a visit this morning. I aim to find him. And to do that, I need to let my men know, and create a task force." He pulls back, giving me space to breathe.

I cup my hands to stop the shaking. "You're saying we have a serial killer?"

He frowns, palms folding over my shoulders. "I shouldn't have told you. I'm sorry. It's just…you're one of the few people in this town I trust. And I guess I want to warn you, too. Because I have a witness who says Chopper's bike wasn't here this morning. So don't go lying for anyone, and don't think this den behind you isn't full of vipers because I know men like these and if it suits them, they'll hurt whoever they have to hurt. Even their fiercest and most loyal female."

"I'm not lying," I whisper, defending Chopper even though the words aren't true. I have no idea where he was this morning, but I do know he wasn't lying in wait for Samantha to leave so he could follow her and cut out her heart. "Chopper's been with me all day. I needed some air this morning so he took me for a ride, that's why whoever your witness is didn't see his bike." I glance over Chief's shoulder to the window Matt is missing from. "Who told you Chopper wasn't here?"

He takes his hands off me. "Someone as stupid as you're being right now. Guess I shouldn't be surprised that your old boyfriend was here this morning; after all, you just don't know when to quit." He glares at me. "You should have quit Warren before you ever let that get started."

My pulse quickens. Warren isn't allowed in this bar, let alone in the back lot. "Warren's barely a mechanic, yet you're the one who gave him a city contract, so I'd say I'm the smarter of the two of us, Chief."

His nostrils flare. "I wouldn't hire him to clean my toilet, so you can thank the mayor for giving Warren that contract."

I remain quiet and Chief's eyes narrow. "We found Samantha's car at the Wiggly Pig. Is that where you went shopping with Gary and Chopper today?" The gleam in his eyes says he already knows it is. He leans toward me. "Whose idea was it to go there instead of Foodville? I bet I can tell you. The man who wanted to see if Samantha's car had been found because if it had, he'd know we already found her body. Think on that tonight because when you bring Gary to the station in the morning, I want your official statement, too. Be smart about who you decide to defend."

By morning, Gary and I will have our stories straight. A story that keeps Chopper in the clear too, because another thing Chief has wrong is *who* suggested we shop at the Wiggly Pig for tomorrow's club barbecue instead of going to Foodville like we usually do. The Wiggly Pig is more of a local place, good for beer and hotdogs, but they don't keep much by way of fresh meat and produce so unless we're packing up for a day on the river, the shopping is done at Foodville. This morning, Gary *insisted* on the Wiggly Pig.

I traverse the stairs to the apartments in a haze of thoughts that don't want to connect. Gary had a reason for wanting to go to the Wiggly Pig, something about the manager trying to get the Grille's business. But what's Warren's reason for framing Chopper? My ex hasn't been allowed to step foot in this bar for three years and he's only returned to living in town full time this past year, when he showed up miraculously able to afford a chunk of land out on Old Route Three. Shortly after that, the walls of his shiny new garage went up. Shortly after that, we heard rumors of the contract he landed, making him the mechanic for all the public works and police vehicles. A curious thing considering one of the reasons he made himself scarce to begin with was to flee charges in an armed robbery he and my cousin Jessop somehow managed to weasel out of.

Slipping inside Gary's apartment, I walk over to his bedroom door. He's sound asleep. Passed out, more like. "How's he doing?" I ask Chopper, who's sitting at the oval dining table shuffling cards and splaying them out for a game of solitaire.

"Bad."

I sit across from him where I have a view into Gary's bedroom. "We've got problems. And Chief thinks that problem is you." He looks up but doesn't say anything. I stare into his smoke-blue eyes, think about the way he's touched me, and I *know* his hands aren't capable of doing what Chief described. I don't think any of the Leidolf are. "Gary is supposed to go down to the station to give a statement tomorrow, but Gary isn't the one Chief is gunning for. He says he has a witness who told him your bike wasn't here after Samantha left this morning. I told him it was because you were with me."

His attention goes back to his game. "Don't get involved."

I flatten my hand over his cards. "Too late for that. Chief also wants my statement tomorrow, and that statement is going to heavily involve your whereabouts between the hours of seven and ten this morning. Chief's pegging you as Samantha's heart-stealing murderer."

He swipes my hand away, aiming to play a card on his ten of spades. I flick my wrist, scattering the cards across the floor. "We need to get our stories straight. Were you here this morning or not?"

He pushes his chair back, nodding to the cards as if I'm going to pick them up. "Don't lie for me." He nods to the cards again.

I fold my arms across my chest. "I would pick them up, but I'm too busy cleaning up your *other* mess."

"I've got it covered."

"Do you now?" I stand and pace to Gary's room, softly shutting the door before going back to lean into Chopper's face. "*Warren* is the one saying you weren't here. My ex, who suddenly got himself in tight with the *mayor*. Still feel covered, Chops? Because Chief feels differently."

He doesn't flinch. His unreadable stare steady. Chopper rarely shows emotion in any part of his body. It's why those handful of nights I've spent with him are so cherished. They allowed me to see him in a different context and helped me to understand what lies beneath this man's unaffected façade.

Straightening, I run a hand through my long brown locks. It's humid out so my hair is a weird mix of waves and curls with a dash of frizz. It always amazes me that it looks like that but manages to remain soft to the touch. Each time I've fallen asleep next to Chopper, I've woken with his face pressed into the thick mass at the back of my neck, his arm snaked over me and his fingers tangled in my locks on the other side. I take a calming breath and drop to my knees, picking up his cards. "You're not a murderer. You don't slice up women and throw them in rivers. So what are we going to do about Warren's accusation, because there's not a chance in Hades that I'm not going to fight for you. So what story are we going with?"

He gets out of his chair and stoops beside me, helping me gather the deck, his fingers brushing over mine as he takes the cards I hold. He meets my eyes, then gets up, plops back into his seat and shuffles the cards, returning to his game. Anger surges through me. "Are you listening to me? I said Chief is gunning for you! And Warren is working some kind of angle that's implicating you. We need to find out what he's up to and get Chief off all our backs!"

His eyes lift, the glint sending chills through me. "Go to Chief. Be truthful. Then stay out of it."

Tears fill my eyes. "Fine, Chopper. Go down for Samantha's murder, and let them book you for the other four, too."

A wrinkle cuts across the corner of his temples. He doesn't know about the others. "Not so big and brave now, are you?"

Only his lips move. "Who?"

I shrug. "Other than Layla, Chief didn't say. He only said the others are similar mutilations. He thinks the same person who killed Layla has been killing ever since, and that his latest victim is Samantha. *You* being that killer."

He turns back to his cards. "Stay close."

My teeth clench. "*I'm* not the one you should be worried about."

He plays a two of hearts. "You heard me."

I shove the cards off the table again. "While you pick those up, I'm going to go check on Samantha's mom. Then I'll put all my efforts into keeping *Gary* out of jail, you know, since you've got yourself covered and all."

~5~

I've never been afraid to walk around Hinton. All my life, I've done so with reckless abandon because I know this place like the back of my hand. But when I walked away from Chopper earlier, I had a second thought about heading out on my own. Chopper had the same thought because Rick was leaning against my Highlander when I got to it. He hopped in the passenger seat as soon as I unlocked the doors. Before we left the parking lot, nine bikes had fallen in behind us. The club is sending their respects to Samantha's mom, and their notification to the killer; Samantha was one of their own, as am I, and now the descendants of the wolf will hunt.

Samantha's mom lives on a corner lot in the back of a trailer park. Pink flamingos dot the flower beds around her steps and colorful little gnomes poke out from various places all along her trailer's underpinning. Instead of looking junky, it's cute. Norma Kay has a way of making old pop cans look fancy. And she never seems to age, just as vibrant today as the first time I remember seeing her behind a concession stand at the Little League field. Her smile lights up a room, and I feel the loss of it today.

One by one, the members of the Leidolf enter Norma Kay's living room, bend a knee in front of her, and offer their condolences. They make her no promises but their meaning is clear. They *will* avenge her daughter.

After the parade of men ends, Rick remains in the house while I sit next to Norma Kay on the oatmeal-colored sofa, taking her hands in mine. "Nothing we say or do can take away your devastation, but we're at your command. Whatever you need, whenever you need it, you have my and Gary's numbers." I nod to Rick. "You can also call the Grille anytime, and one of the guys will answer."

She gives my hands a squeeze. "Every time Samantha started using again, I knew it was only a matter of time. But when she was clean…"

This poor woman was on a high of her own, thinking her daughter was finally on her way to a long and happy drug-free life. "Gary won't rest until he finds the person responsible for taking her away from you."

"I know." She sniffs. "I know he loved my Samantha."

While I hold Norma Kay, cry with her, and offer what little comfort there is to give in times when no words or deeds can ease someone else's pain, Rick checks the food supply in the kitchen. Casseroles and meat trays began arriving as soon as word of Samantha's death started to burn through town.

Satisfied Norma Kay won't starve if hunger breaks through her suffering, he inspects the doors and windows and does a search in Samantha's room. She didn't stay here often and Norma Kay said Chief had already rummaged through the room, but Rick disappears into the space anyway. When he emerges, he manages to look a lot like Chopper. Unreadable.

Outside, the Leidolf fan out through the trailer park community. The people who live in this particular court are mostly older, and older people like to talk. The club likes to listen.

~

"Anything?" I ask as Rick and I exit the trailer, addressing my question to him and the others. Several headshakes answer me. I look around. The neighbors are all abuzz on their porches, the haze of light from both inside and outside the trailers brightening up the night. A terrible notion snakes through me. "Someone needs to stay here. Watch who comes and goes, and kick anyone out who gives Norma Kay the creeps. I've heard of killers stalking their victim's family, and Samantha likely knew the person who attacked her." I meet their faces one by one. "Which means we're likely to know them, too."

Rick nods, confirming the club is way ahead of my instincts. "We'll have eyes on Norma Kay, and we'll make sure she isn't bothered by well-wishers who talked trash about Samantha when she was alive."

"Thanks." I give him half a smile and press a hand to my stomach. Norma Kay was adamant that she didn't want fake people traipsing through her house; that removes at least half the town from her guest list because people can't help talking about every single bad thing a person has ever done, flipping a switch at death to then act as if the person was their best friend. So whoever patrols the trailer will have their work cut out for them in making sure no one overstays a welcome they were never given to begin with. But it's the idea that the person next to me at the grocery store could be a cold-blooded killer that has me lightheaded. "We'll need to cancel tomorrow's barbecue. No one is going to feel like celebrating the first day of summer anymore."

"Already canceled, little darlin'." Rick opens my car door. "Hop in and let's get back to the bar. The club has business, and Gary's up. He wants to talk to you."

~

Pulling into the lot behind the bar, I park next to Chopper's bike. Most members of the Leidolf ride Harleys, and like the man himself, Chopper's Black Mamba Buell 1190SX stands out. There's no mistaking his stunning machine. Not even to the average person who has a hard time distinguishing between any of the men's bikes. When Chopper is out in town, people notice. Which means if he wasn't at the bar when Samantha was murdered, someone knows where he was. It's going to come down to whether or not they can prove what their eyes saw.

Taking the steps two at a time, I enter Gary's apartment to find him sitting on the couch, head in hands and a bottle of Jack Daniels on the coffee table in front of him. Tennessee honey. The whiskey that's sure to make you forget all your woes. If those woes don't include a gutted girlfriend with a missing heart.

Sitting beside him, I run an arm around his shoulders. "Norma Kay is holding up. Randy stayed with her."

He stares at the bottle of Jack. "Four others?"

I look up at Chopper. He's watching us from his spot at the table, the deck of cards stacked neatly in front of him. "Chief says he's putting together a task force because he thinks it's a serial killer. But I'm not so sure he's going to *hunt* so much as frame. He's got theories."

Gary reaches forward, tipping the bottle toward an empty glass. He hands me the drink. "Warren is giving me an alibi."

Time freezes. Both men stare at me, Gary urging the whiskey toward my lips. I smack the glass away. He keeps it from spilling and downs the drink himself. "I didn't ask Warren to do this. He went and did it on his own, and now it's done. He'll stick with his story, and *I'll* take care of Chopper's alibi."

"Warren." I whisper his name. "You're in contact with Warren?"

Gary sets the empty glass beside the bottle and pinches the bridge of his nose, ignoring my question. "We'll go down to see Chief in the morning. You answer his questions truthfully. Then you stick close to the club until this is over."

"You're in contact with Warren?" I say louder.

His bloodshot eyes turn to mine. "What I'm saying to you isn't a request. You see Chief, you tell your truth, and then you keep your head down while the club handles this situation."

I shove myself to standing. "I might not be a kutte-wearing member but I'm not some little girl you're going to stuff into a corner either. If you won't tell me how Warren got in the middle of your alibi, I'll find out for myself."

I stomp to the door and Gary's voice pricks over me. "Stay out of this, Tessa. And leave Warren alone. Or I *will* put you in a corner."

~6~

Before leaving Riverside Grille, more than one club member told me to "stay close," like I'm some cat prone to wandering off. I get that they're spooked, word of the other murders I told Chopper about already spread through their ranks, but I can't breathe under their roof. Not when Gary's openly admitting to being in contact with Warren and *ordering* me to leave Warren alone. Like Warren isn't the last person on this earth that I'd willingly speak to. Like Gary should be doing *anything* with Warren other than punching him in the face.

When I leave the bar late, it's normal for the Leidolf to either follow me or give me a ride home. And I can't say it's abnormal for them to drive by my house at all hours. I even replaced the door lock with one that has buttons, giving the club the code so the wolves can come and go as they please, but none of them use it. They respect my personal space and ask before entering. The fact that Zeno followed me home and is now parked outside means he's under orders. The club is guarding me.

Beth peeks out the window, shivering as she moves the curtain aside one tiny inch. "Why is he sitting out there?"

I pour a glass of Ricard, slide it onto the counter for her and drink straight from the bottle. I was hoping she wouldn't be here tonight. That she'd be shacking up with her on-again, off-again boyfriend Arnold so that I'd have the place to myself. I want to be alone. But Beth and Arnold's romance never lasts long. She'll say she's going to move in with him and when it comes right down to it, she's back to *renting* my spare room. Labeling it that way herself even though there's not been a single time in the last four years when she's offered to pay a dime toward anything. Not the water, not the power, and she only goes to the store when I don't stock the cabinets for her. Then she only buys *special* things, being sure to tell me about them which translates to me needing to keep my hands off her stuff. "Have a drink, and get real used to the club being here."

She drops the curtain, walking the short pace to the kitchen with a smile on her full lips. "I guess I am used to you bringing home those strays, but why is he outside? Lover's spat?"

I should kick her out. After all, she's the older sister. *She* should be helping *me* out, not promising she'll pay rent *this time* when she knows good and well all she's going to do is give me lip service. But our roles have always been reversed. I've always felt the need to look out for her. Sure, when we were kids she used to pretend she was my savior. That she was clever when it came to hiding from Dad, when all she did was plead for me to go with her into places we had no way of escaping. Even then, I'd feel bad for her and give in when she begged. Each and every time we were found. When I was left alone, able to get out of the house before she got her paws on me, no one ever caught me.

Beth also liked to fix my hair, treat me like her little doll and take credit for me. I hated every second of it but more than disliking my hair being pulled and standing around *looking pretty* while she tried to get me to show off for whoever would pay us any attention, I hated to see her pout. I hated how hard everything seemed for her. You still don't have to look long to see her pain, how she feels less than. Less than what, I don't know. She's just never been able to get enough wind under her wings to fly. Me, I bought a wind machine and made my own air. *I* control my own fate. I won't leave it up to others. Not even Gary.

I pick up the glass and shove it at Beth. She takes it and I plop myself down at the dinette table in my eat-in kitchen, still clutching my bottle of Ricard. Beth's face falls as I turn the bottle up. She sighs and sits across from me. "I guess he's out there because of what happened to Samantha?"

I nod, looking around my kitchen and remembering all the plans I had for this place. Refinish the cabinets, install new drawer pulls and replace the Formica countertop. Small-budget improvements that will add big value. Now, renovating seems trivial.

My little house is perched atop the hillside overlooking the river. This part of town is old, many of the houses rundown. I found one with good bones and a private backyard. The previous owners went to great lengths to plant rhododendrons around the inside perimeter of the knee-high stone wall marking my property. It's only a third of an acre and the main road is practically right outside my front door, but beyond that is the river. Beyond that is the train track, the noise from which you learn to tune out after a while. I rarely register hearing it. What I do hear is the sound of Beth's questions. I'm not surprised she learned about the brutality of Samantha's death, it's the answers she thinks I can give her that are the problem. She expects me to have an inside scoop and after what Chief told me about the murders, I guess I do. But I came home to escape. Not to relive the images Chief planted in my mind.

I weigh telling her about the other murders. I love my sister, but she doesn't keep secrets and when she doesn't have one to tell, she makes one up. Her loose lips aren't exactly known for repeating accurate information, either. She'd rather have something to say than nothing, and she likes to talk. Still, if there's a serial killer in our town and Samantha wasn't just a one-and-done, Beth needs to know. So do all the other women. "The way Samantha was killed is familiar to Chief." I meet her eyes. "He thinks a serial killer is walking our streets."

Her face blanches, mouth frozen in the shape of the last words she was forming, eyes wide and fingers trembling enough to send tiny waves of Ricard crashing off the sides of the glass in her grip.

I throw back a swig of my own bottle and she follows suit, gulping a mouthful and making a face as it slides down her throat.

"That body found just outside of town four years ago? He says it *was* Layla." I take another big drink, more of a drinker than Beth so I don't need to make a face, I only need to numb the fear quaking through my veins. "Been a murder every year since, just over our borders and now right in our own back yard." I offer to top off her glass and she shakes her head. "Don't worry, sis. You and I are fine. The Leidolf are on it!" I shove my bottle triumphantly into the air, tongue heavy on the slurred words.

She swallows. "*You* don't have to worry. But none of the Leidolf like me. I might as well put a sign on my back and let the killer know I'm a sitting duck."

I drain more of my bottle, closing my eyes so I don't have to look at her. We've had this argument before. Not about the killer, but about whether or not people in this town like her. She insists she's treated like an outsider, but she isn't. And none of the Leidolf dislike her. She rarely comes into the bar and when any of them come here, she disappears into her room, so they've never been around her enough to have an opinion on her. And they don't really care why she's standoffish. As far as they're concerned, the fewer "straights" interacting with them, the better. Which is why the restaurant part of the bar was tricky. A different type of clientele shows up for breakfast and lunch; people who wouldn't be caught patronizing a "biker bar". They sure show up for earlier mealtimes though, because deep down inside all the hypocrites lives a person who *wants* to walk close to danger. I've overheard some of them talking about coming to Riverside Grille, saying it proudly as if it makes them *street cool*. "I should punch them in the face."

Beth's nose crinkles. "You're going to punch a killer in the face?"

I point my bottle at her, the woozy sway of a stellar buzz rocking me gently. "People like you. Won't come into the bar and talk trash about my boys."

She pushes her glass to the side. "I don't come in there because of my job. I doubt the parents I babysit for would want to hire a nanny who hangs out with a biker gang."

I slam my bottle on the table. "They're not a gang!"

She gets up. "Yeah, well, you're drunk. So I'm going to go tell your little friend outside to come get your stupid gun from the nightstand before you go shooting people for calling a *gang* of motorcycle *thugs* a *gang!*"

~7~

Beth never finished high school. She always struggled—with grades and friends. The day she turned sixteen she dropped out for good. The Robertsons hired her as a nanny for their four kids, even giving her the spare room above their garage so she'd be on call for them, due to them both being RNs and also part of the volunteer fire department. Beth took to that kind of work and before long she was running a sort of daycare in the Robertson's big backyard. Parents would schedule *play dates* and drop off their kids with five dollars tucked into their lunch bags.

She's basically still running illegal daycares, sometimes allowing parents to drop off their kids at one of the houses where she regularly babysits. Her rates have gone up over the years but unlike certified daycares, she has no overhead, so comparatively, she's still a bargain. That's a win for parents and allows Beth to make a livable wage—adjusting for the fact that all she pays for is her car and clothes addiction. She doesn't even pay her car insurance. Mom does that.

I lumber into the living room, dawn having come and gone while I slept off last night's binge. Randy is sitting on the couch, his kutte draped over the back and his socked feet resting on the rug underneath him. I raise a brow. "What did you do to get stuck on night watch?"

He removes my pistol from his waistband and places it on the coffee table in front of him. I groan. "If I wanted to go on a shooting spree, I'd do it sober."

A smile spreads over his lips and he turns away, getting off the couch, his white t-shirt tightening on his biceps as he stretches. He's the oldest member of Gary's charter but Randy doesn't look like any grandpa I've ever seen. He acts like one, though. The boots I wear nearly every day came from him, a birthday gift last year. Samantha was always flipping through magazines, bringing them into the bar and leaving them on the counter when she was finished. Instead of trashing a fancy clothing one, I flipped through it and snapped a picture of the black lace-up riding boots I'd never splurge on. Randy saw, and he bought them for me.

He slips on his kutte and grabs his shoes from the mat beside the door. Beth walks by me, entering the kitchen without a word to either of us. I follow her. "You seriously went and told them I was going to harm someone?"

She starts a pot of coffee, remaining silent for enough beats to let me know she's still mad. "I told the one who was out there that you were drunk and possibly going to hurt yourself. Ten minutes later, the second one came through the door. No knocking. No asking. He just came in and curiously knew exactly where your gun was." She faces me. "Then he didn't leave. No asking if I was okay with a strange man in the house. He just plopped himself right down and started shedding his clothes."

I shrug. "You shouldn't have gone outside being a drama queen."

She turns back to her coffee, filling a cup half full of cream while she waits for the pot to be ready. "The problem is you installing those keypad locks instead of having deadbolts with normal keys. Then they wouldn't be able to barge in whenever they feel like."

I take a pitcher of water from the refrigerator. She knows good and well that I installed the keypads so the club *could* come and go as they please. "Just be glad you didn't call Randy a gang member to his face."

She grunts while I chug the water, face losing its indignance as she pours her coffee and begins to stir. "Marla from down at the post office said she heard that Samantha was beaten to death, *then* sliced open like a frog in science class."

"How would she know?"

Her shoulders bob. "Her nephew Darren is a fireman."

"He's fifteen. Darren might get to ride on a firetruck, but I doubt they'd let him see a body."

She spins around, as if looking at me will sway my opinion. "Marla said what he saw made him throw up all over the inside of Bobby Baker's truck."

"Good. Bobby's a tool."

She frowns. "After he puked, Darren heard Bobby tell someone on the phone that Samantha was *raped*."

I'd guessed as much but hearing it out loud is sickening, even coming from a questionable source. "Bobby spends too much time chasing skirts to know what's under one so I doubt he could tell."

"Bobby's nice." She defends him.

"Bobby is a dirtbag and suspect number one if you ask me."

Her laugh is dry. "Suspect number one has to be Gary. That's why Chief came to talk to you, right?"

I rub my eyes, yesterday's events flooding back in with overwhelming clarity. I have to go down to the station soon. "Chief knows it wasn't Gary. Our cousin isn't violent. No one I know is. Not like that."

"What about Warren?" she whispers.

My heart misses a beat. I stare at her. "What about him?"

She chews her lip, the way she always does when she's nervous. "I'm not saying he's *violent*, but he likes it rough. At least, he liked it that way with me."

~8~

Growing up, Warren was my best friend. Our parents didn't get along but we never let their petty feud bleed onto us. Not even after I turned into another one of those small-town beauties and my parents decided they could monetize my face. I wasn't regarded quite as highly as Layla but they didn't let that deter their dreams of fame and fortune. And I didn't let their insistence that Warren wasn't good enough for me deter my dream of being his.

Back then, what I knew was that before the darling little nose, big wide eyes and high cheekbones, all I ever got at home was yelled at. If I missed one question on a test I was berated for being an idiot, and if I didn't miss any, they'd say "So? Anyone can do that." Mind you, no one in my family ever even graduated high school. Not my parents, aunts, uncles, siblings or older cousins. I was the first. That's why I never cared what anyone thought of Warren. No one around me was any better than him, and in most cases, they were worse.

When my friendship with Warren turned into more, I thought he'd be mine forever. That I'd be his. That the dreams we talked about and the plans we made would one day come true. But he betrayed me, and while I was busy pulling *that* knife out of my back, he slept with my sister.

Beth's a lightweight when it comes to alcohol and she was drunk when Warren took advantage of her. She bumped into him at a speakeasy over in Sprague, a place far away from here where she could drink without being near the Leidolf. Not one to ever garner much male attention, she was flattered when Warren started chatting her up and buying her drinks. As much as I hate him, I can't deny how sexy he is. He hit puberty early and it did his body *good*. Corded muscle over long, sunbaked arms. Big rough hands. Legs sculpted as if he's one of those Greek statues come to life. And as he aged from boy to man, he only got better. Beth never had a chance. Once his mouth started working over her neck and he whispered in her ear how much he'd always wanted her, she had no other option than to cave.

I know what it feels like to have Warren's hands on you. His mouth. It's why I gathered all the little envelopes of money Gary had sent me over the years and gave them to Warren when he turned sixteen. His birthday is two months before mine and we had our eye on a van, something that would be ours and give us a place to be together. The van was put in his name only, and the back of it is where he took Beth all these years later. He slept with her right on top of all my memories.

I press a palm to my stomach, never failing to feel ill when forced to recall Beth's tearful confession. She hates herself for what she did with Warren that night and has shot down all the passes he's made at her since. And that's one story of hers that I believe because several people have mentioned how she practically runs in the opposite direction whenever Warren shows up in her vicinity. They mean it to be a compliment, one sister scorned equaling two, but they don't know the real reason she avoids him. The very fact she's managed to keep such juicy details to herself is a testament to how bad she feels for being a part of that particular betrayal. There are plenty of others, both things gossiped about that I've actually done and ones she's just made up, but the whole of them combined isn't as bad as Warren telling her he was only with me because I was as close as he could get to her.

I find my nearly empty bottle of Ricard and drain what's left of it. "You're right, Beth. Warren is dirtbag suspect number two."

She takes the empty bottle from me. "I don't think Bobby or Warren are likely suspects, but I hope Chief figures out who is before you drink yourself to death."

I pat her cheek. "I can always count on you to exaggerate. Just remember what kind of company your overreacting got you last night."

She glances toward our now empty living room. "Do you think Samantha died before... I mean, it would be a blessing, right? To be gone *before* you get cut open like that?"

Samantha's smiling face pops into my mind. Even at her worst, she always managed to have that smile. "I'm going to go talk to Chief, see what his plan is for warning people."

"You think he's going to announce there's a serial killer on the loose?"

I shrug. "People already seem to know how Samantha was killed, so even if Chief keeps the other murders quiet for a while, people are going to be scared. And they have a right to know that they *should* be afraid."

She nods. "Especially the female people."

I'm struck with another fear when Beth moves to the sink, leans back and runs her fingers through her coarse blonde hair--such a stark contrast to my own dark locks. Of all the women in this town, I'd wager I'm the safest. Beth is the complete opposite of me. "You should go stay with Arnold for a while."

Her eyes narrow. "Living in this one-horse town when I'm twenty-six and unmarried is hard enough without you joining the witch hunt trying to force me into marrying a man I can't stand half the time."

I cup my hands over her shoulders. "No one is erecting gallows in the town square and I'm not telling you to marry Arnold, though he'd love for you to, and you know he'd treat you like his queen. But unless you want a club member camping in the living room every night, you need to go someplace safe. I don't want you staying here alone."

"I won't be alone if you come home at night." Her eyes dart to the floor and back up. "You know people talk. You're at the bar every night, staying there with…well, no one really knows *who* you're waking up with, so they *talk*."

I drop my hands from her shoulders. I have no doubt people around here think I'm sleeping with every single member of the Leidolf. I wouldn't put it past some of the finger-pointing gossipmongers to include Gary in their tallies. "First off, I work several jobs in the bar so of course I'm always there. Second, even if I was home in my own bed every night, people would still talk. That's what bored little rumor spreaders do, they flap their jaws for no good reason instead of getting busy with their own lives." I pull a to-go cup from the cabinet and pour some of her coffee into it. "I'm going to go get busy with *my* life, which doesn't include standing here giving gossip a breath of my time."

She sighs. "I'm only telling you what your behavior looks like to outsiders. I know you wouldn't sleep with any of those…men." I roll my eyes at her and she smiles. "I could rip out all your hair and even slick as an eight ball, every man in this town would still fall all over themselves just to get you to look at them. So why do you think insurance boy isn't on his knees yet?"

I put the lid on my coffee. "According to you, it's because I'm banging all the members of the Leidolf." I head toward my bedroom, anger pressing against the walls of my being. If Beth didn't start this particular rumor, she certainly encouraged it. I can hear her now, waltzing into the post office and just happening to mention how she hasn't seen me because I didn't come home *again* last night. "Go to Arnold's, Beth. And marry him!"

~9~

Our police department has been operating out of the same building for longer than I've been alive. They've made updates over the years and have twice relocated into a row of trailers after floodwaters rose high enough to breach this old brick building that's cut from the same era as the bar. But they always return to the plaster walls and narrow halls.

There's a lot of community support for our law enforcement and it shows when it comes time for budgets to be written. But somehow, that money never seems to manifest. Not according to the officers who frequent the bar. They rarely get pay increases and any new influx of budget dollars gets spent well before it can trickle down to make a difference in the way they do their jobs. The new vests they all own were gained by an apple butter fundraiser put on by the Pentecostal Church. The Baptists, not wanting to be outdone, sold hotdogs to purchase two new uniforms for each officer in the department. These sales always take place over holiday weekends when we're likely to have out-of-towners rolling through to fish or float along the two rivers that join at the mouth of town. One river is slow and lazy, the other is rough and whitecapped—the water a metaphor for the people who live along the shores. We're easygoing, until we're not.

Waiting in a room by myself, separated from Gary to give the *statement* Chief wants, I feel the change in my temperament coming on. In contrast to the seeming insignificance of Layla's death, her murder causing little more than a rustling of lips,

Samantha's death is rousing wolf and law alike, and it's a shame it took four other murders to shine a spotlight on the ripple that began with Layla. It's a *shame* that Chief never confirmed that the beheaded body was even Layla's. Someone in town might have had information about her last known whereabouts and stopped a killer long before he got his hands on Samantha.

"Sorry to keep you waiting." Chief sits down across from me.

I fold my arms. "Let's just hope no other women were murdered while you did." The frown lines in the corner of his mouth deepen. I sigh. "I assume you've been interrogating Gary?"

He flips open the folder of papers he brought in with him. "I'm not interrogating anyone. Yet." He slides a blank sheet of paper across the table to me. "I need you to write down your activities from the morning Samantha was found, specifically who you saw, when you saw them, and *where* you saw them."

I shake my head. "I see a lot of people, can't keep it all straight."

He rests his hands atop the folder, lacing his fingers together. "Tessa, don't make this harder than it needs to be. Just tell me where you were that morning and who was with you so I can get on with finding who murdered Samantha. That girl was a lot of things, but she didn't deserve what was done to her."

"Obviously." I roll my eyes.

He leans back in his chair, unclasping his hands and shuffling to the next page in his folder. "Here's what I know. Warren stayed at the bar the night before. He got drunk downstairs, so Gary let him sleep it off upstairs."

Lie. I'm not going to say it out loud, but Gary would never let Warren inside the bar, let alone upstairs. Even *if* the two of them are suddenly close enough to be handing out alibis.

Chief continues. "Though I don't care much for your old boyfriend, Warren is vouching for Gary's whereabouts the next morning and Gary is confirming Warren was in an apartment upstairs." He slides another paper across the desk. "Here's Gary's statement. Go on. Read it." He taps Gary's signature at the bottom. "Your ex and your cousin have matching stories. Warren was in the hallway when Samantha slipped out of Gary's apartment. After she left, he knocked on Gary's door to thank him, and Gary invited Warren in for breakfast. Seems they had themselves a nice little meal while Samantha was being cut open."

The room spins. I suck air through my nose. Chief circles the table and kneels beside me, bringing a trashcan with him. "Tessa, honey, I don't know if Warren and Gary are full of it or if they're telling the truth. What I do know is there's a killer in our town. He may or may not be someone you care about, but I know you loved Samantha. Help me find who hurt her by not lying to me about what you saw that morning."

My head is reeling. I shouldn't be surprised that Gary and Warren have matching statements, Gary would have made sure they did. But *I* could have been his alibi. We don't need Warren. "I was with Chopper—"

"No, you weren't!" Chief cuts me off. "And you've never been a liar so don't start now. Don't break every faith I've ever had in you by trying to protect someone who doesn't need your help."

I look down to where he's still kneeling beside me, resolve strengthening. "Chopper was with me."

He gets up and leaves the room. I sit with my eyes on Gary's paper, his chicken scratch spelling out what he ate with Warren that morning. Brown sugar cinnamon oatmeal and bacon. A typical breakfast for Gary.

The door swings open and Gary strolls in, dropping his frame into the seat Chief had first sat in. "Do what I told you to do, Tessa. Write down the *truth*, and then go wait for me in the Highlander."

I shove his statement at him. "You want truth? How about the truth of you betraying me? You let Warren into the bar, didn't you? Had him *upstairs* where I could have stumbled into the same apartment as him." He stares at me. My heart pounds, bile rising into the back of my throat. "Of all the people who would betray me, I *never* thought it would be you."

His eyes cut deep. His words even further. "Write down your statement, and then wait outside." He gets up and opens the door, Chief standing on the other side waiting.

"What about Chopper?" I ask Gary's back. "Is this what we're doing now? Abandoning each other?"

"Do as you're told, Tessa. And do it now!" Gary slams the door.

I sit perfectly still until Chief walks back in, the same solemn look on his face that he's had all day. "The state medical examiner is going to have Samantha's body for a while. But once it's released and she's buried, things will get a little easier for your cousin."

"Unless you frame him for murder." I grab the blank sheet of paper he gave me earlier. "Oh, wait, it's Chopper you're trying to frame." In big letters, I fill the page, writing: **Chopper did not kill Samantha.**

Leaving the paper on the table, I get up. "I'm going to go wait in my vehicle before I get yelled at again by your co-conspirator. You have yourself a real nice day now, *Chief.*"

~10~

Chopper, Rick, Zeno, and Randy were waiting outside the police station. I didn't speak to any of them, though Gary did briefly before getting behind the wheel of my Highlander. From the police station to the bar, we remained silent.

Gary took hold of my arm in the parking lot, fingers tightening around my bicep to force me through the door and up the stairs to his apartment. He's never put his hands on me like this before, but today I'm guaranteed to have a bruising memento of his grip.

Chopper follows us into the apartment and shuts the door. Gary sits on the couch and pulls me down beside him, his grip loosening. "I'm not throwing Chopper under a bus, and I'm sure as heck not abandoning you." His arm slips around me. "Warren *wasn't* here."

I let out a breath of tension. He does the same. "Warren got the call to come tow a vehicle to the impound lot. When he arrived at the Wiggly Pig, he saw it was Samantha's car and overheard some of the officers talking. He heard enough to know her body was…freshly killed, and that I was the prime suspect. Then he heard the part about her heart being missing and he panicked. He spoke to Chief in a daze, saying he'd just left my place when the tow call came in."

I stare at the floor. "Warren is who you were on the phone with when Chief got here?"

Gary's hand tightens on my shoulder. "He was trying to warn me, let me get ahead of the news."

I slide to the far end of the couch, away from his reach. "Warren gave you an alibi that won't hold water if anyone checks into his actual whereabouts, which is God knows where with that run-around dirtbag. And he also threw Chopper straight under the wheels of the bus. Warren is not your *friend*, Gary. He's not helping you, and I highly doubt he panicked. Warren sat on the wall eavesdropping like the dirty little rat he is and made a plan. There's something in this for him, and apparently that something has to do with getting rid of Chopper."

Chopper looks up, a smile on his face. I throw an empty beer can at him. He laughs, catching the can and giving me a look that sets my belly on fire. Gary puts a phone in the center of the coffee table. "Chopper was with Alice the night Samantha stayed with me. Alice came here with Sam, but she didn't leave with her. Chops took her home a little earlier so she could get ready for work, and…" He glances at me. "He was at her place long enough for a few neighbors to see his bike leave. He came straight here and the camera out front shows him coming in seven minutes after Sam left. He's clear. So next time I tell you to do something, you do it. Don't question me ever again, especially in front of others."

Chopper's eyes are now down, the smile wiped off his face. We're not a couple and I'm not jealous, but it's still awkward that I've been trying to defend him when the whole time he had a different woman to alibi him. A great big busty one with more curves than a West Virginia backroad.

I face Gary. "If you would have just told me from the start that Chopper had an alibi instead of telling me not to worry about someone I love, then I wouldn't have bucked you. I would have backed you, just like I always do. But you're not telling me anything. You're keeping me in the dark while you whisper on the phone with *Warren*. I may not be a member of the club but

I'd take a bullet for every one of you and I guarantee you that's something your new little buddy wouldn't do."

His jaw ticks. "I share blood with you, but even without that, we're family. My brothers all know it, and you being willing to take a bullet for us is part of the problem, Tessa."

I stab a finger into my chest. "Oh, so it's *my* fault a serial killer is on the loose? Because I'm too loyal? Thanks for clearing that up."

He rolls his eyes right back at me and looks at Chopper, who nods. Gary runs a hand down his face. "Despite the connections Chief is making, I'm not convinced Samantha was murdered by a serial killer. I think her death is an attack against the club."

I shake my head. "Who would attack the club?"

He snorts. "Plenty of people. And that's why I don't want you in the middle of this. I want you to help me plan Samantha's service, and I might have some other errands for you, but unless I ask, you stay away from everything that has anything to do with these murders." He pins me with a look. "And you do as I say. Got it?"

I lean my elbows on my knees, processing his speculation. "She was mutilated, Gary. Just like the other women."

"Chief let me look at the files he's been putting together on the others. None of them were missing a heart."

I swallow. "So you think the person took her heart because you loved her with all of yours?"

His eyes brim red. "I think whoever hurt her knows I love you, too."

Chopper lifts his eyes. "Sam was just easier for them to get to."

My blood runs cold. I could be dead right now, my heart cut out and what's left of my body being combed over by the medical examiner. Instead of Samantha's funeral, Gary could be planning mine. His warm hand stretches to rest on my back.

"I've got to go out to where Sam's car was found and search for surveillance cameras. Stay here in the bar until I get back."

Fear presses against my lungs. "I want to go with you." His mouth twists up into what's sure to be a no and I slide close to his side. "Please? I can help get people to open up without you having to ignite your short fuse."

"People do like to talk to her." I hear the smile in Chopper's voice.

Gary rubs a hand over my hair. "The town sweetheart, and a huge pain in my backside. Go tell Rick you're coming with me. He was a little too happy earlier when I told him he was on Tessa duty for the rest of the day."

~11~

Samantha parked at the Wiggly Pig but she wasn't carved up in the lot. After Gary *speaks* to the manager, we're allowed to view footage from the two outside cameras, one wide angle of the back of the building and one on the front where Samantha parked. Of her own accord, she gets out of her car and walks across the pavement to the sidewalk, following it back past the store and down the side of the building until she's out of camera range. The rear camera has a view of the sidewalk but she never walks past. Either she darted across the street, or she got into a car that was parked between the view of the two cameras. After watching the footage from that point until the time when her body was found, without seeing a car emerge from the blind spot, we're working under the assumption that Samantha darted across the street and either entered another building or walked down an alley.

Whatever Samantha was doing that morning, it looks to me like she was doing it with someone she knew. Like maybe she was meeting her drug dealer. Gary says no, and he's normally good at sniffing out when she's back on the pills, but his feelings for her could have blinded him. Chief agrees with me. I called him once we arrived back at the bar, dipping into my office to pick up my shoulder bag. I asked how strongly he still felt about the serial killer angle and he informed me it isn't an angle, it's a fact.

Meandering my way back out into the Grille, I watch the bustle from the archway. Almost everyone can be found in here from time to time, the tinted glass on the bay of windows across

45

the front providing privacy even during the daylight hours when the booths lining that wall are filled with breakfast and lunch patrons. Tonight we're particularly busy, and there's no doubt it's because everyone wants to gather at the watering hole to discuss Samantha.

The sheer number of people isn't the only difference in the bar tonight. The Leidolf aren't milling about like they usually do. They're lined around the perimeter, observing the patrons in a way that has to make the bulk of them feel uncomfortable. Gary opened this place with a vision for it to be a legitimate business. A way for the club to make money while offsetting their image by making their *clubhouse* an open spectacle. His efforts have gone a long way because despite the occasional rowdy crowd, the Leidolf aren't party animals. That I know of, none of them use drugs and they most certainly are never out of control. These men thrive on being in possession of their faculties.

I move to Chopper's end of the bar and clap my hand over his shoulder. "Tell the guys to be nice to the patrons, then come drive me home. I need to check on Beth and she likes you better than the rest."

I walk out the back door, turn down the alleyway toward the front of the building so Zeno isn't staring directly at me, and lean on the building, closing my eyes. The bite of cold that lives somewhere between night and day nips at my nose and I draw the air deep into my lungs. I'm taking Chopper home with me because I'm scared. I'm going home because I'm worried about Beth. *If* Gary is right, someone could take a shot at Beth, which will hurt him by proxy. Even without me in the mix, a crime against her would bother him because at the end of the day she's his cousin, too. And she's also a member of a town under the protection of the Leidolf. That's what these so-called gangsters are—protectors. Even of Beth.

Thing is, I don't think Gary is right. I believe Chief. I believe the information he has about the five bodies proves a serial murderer is operating all around us. Once in our county and once in the other four counties surrounding us. But there's another county that touches ours and right now, thinking about that northern border makes my stomach ache.

"Hey." The soft whisper shakes loose my thoughts. I open my eyes and look at the man standing to my left, his body blocking the alleyway. Matt didn't come in for his usual grease-filled plate of fried okra at lunch. Tina, who'd been busing tables during that time, muttered about his absence because I'm not the only one who thinks he's a slice of pie with a whole scoop of vanilla ice cream melting overtop. He reminds me of one of those GI Joe dolls Beth used to play with. I never could figure out the appeal of playing with bits of plastic but Beth got one thing right, Ken had *nothing* on her beefy soldier dolls.

Matt's also wholesome. Like bread. And everyone knows toast never hurt anyone. I pivot in his direction, keeping one shoulder pressed firmly against the wall. "So you're not mute after all?"

He rubs the back of his neck. "You're always busy so I just…don't bother you."

Pulling myself upright, I pace across the pavement to stand in front of him. "You do know it's creepy to stare at women, right? Makes us super uncomfortable."

His eyes dart away. "Yeah, I just…see you out here sometimes." He nods to the window in what used to be Helen Kizer's store back when she tried to make of go of selling candles. "I'm never sure if I should bother you."

I smile at him and his lips twitch. He shoves his hands into his pockets. "I guess you've heard about that girl by now. The whole town's talking about it. So tonight I…do you need a ride?"

I quirk a brow. "It's a little late for an insurance salesman to be out, isn't it?"

Sweat beads over his forehead. He pulls his hands back out of his pockets and wipes it away with one perfectly sculpted forearm. "I'm not a loser or anything, but I'm living here. In my office." He nods to the window again. "Doesn't seem sensible to rent a place when I'm already paying rent on a building that has a spare room. There's a full bathroom, too. Just no kitchen."

I already know his living situation. Everyone does. "Are you a killer and I'm in stranger danger right now?"

His eyebrows raise. "Just because a man stares, it doesn't mean he's dangerous. It means he looks out his window sometimes just to see if you're out here, and tonight you were, looking like you were thinking really hard on something." He mimics my posture from earlier, leaning his big shoulder on the wall. "I didn't want you to sit out here alone. Then I wondered if your car broke down or something and decided to come see if you need a ride."

Chopper's bike starts up. He's out front, and I know it's his bike because I know the sound of all these bikes. "I have a ride."

He pulls off the wall, glancing down the alleyway toward the front of the building. "Are these guys safe for you to be around?"

I move closer to him. His head swivels back my way, a smile spreading over his face at how close I am. I smile back. "So that's why you avoided your lunch today, you're scared of a few tattoos."

His smile fades, chest puffing and ice-blue eyes standing their ground with mine. "I'm not scared of anyone. My stomach just needs a break from the crap you serve in that bar."

I laugh. "Trust me, if *I* was the one serving it, the food would be much worse."

"Oh, yeah?" He grins. "Then can I have your number? I'll take you out for a nice dinner."

I push by him, heading down the alley. "My number is public record around here. If you want a date, you can find it."

"How do you know I don't already have it and was just being polite?" he calls after me.

Chopper pulls to the mouth of the alley. I hop on his bike, plop the spare helmet on my head and blow Matt a kiss. He stuffs his hands into his pockets, a smile teasing the corner of his delectable mouth. I wrap my arms around Chopper's waist. "I'm going to figure out what that man's smile tastes like real soon."

Chopper's hand slides over mine, pressing my fingers tightly into him. "Make sure your head is right before you jump in with anyone."

"Is that what you're going to tell Alice when she comes begging for another round?" I tease.

He laughs. I don't hear it but I feel it in the way the muscles contract on his abdomen. "It's not what I'll tell the woman who's been bucking the law to defend me," he declares, speeding us off into the darkness. I rest my head on his shoulder as he navigates the streets. He's on the couch tonight, but I might sleep right there curled up next to him.

Beth is an early riser. I stagger out of my bedroom once I hear her come out of her room for the second time, the first being when she went to shower. She stops in the hall between our two rooms, hers being to the left of my door. "Which gang member was here last night?"

I roll my eyes. "Don't start. Especially while Chopper is around."

She sighs, fussing with my bedhead. "He was gone when I got out of the shower or else I wouldn't have said that. He's scary."

"Not as scary as my morning hair." I swat her fingers away from my tangled strands and drop a kiss on her cheek, trying not to think about Warren's lips having been there. And I *know* they were. The man is nothing if not thorough. He would have had himself all over every inch of her.

She follows me into the kitchen, going to the coffee pot while I grab a packet of oatmeal from the box in the cupboard. "Any word on Sam's killer? I'm sure Chief has gone through every member of Gary's gang by now."

"Even the old-timers don't call them that anymore, Beth."

She shrugs. "When Gary first brought them here, they did."

I pop the bowl of oatmeal into the microwave. "Yeah, and now they sit in the bar-turned-café having their eggs cooked to order and their coffee refilled for free." I face her. "Half the people in this town bring me their taxes every year and the other half don't have taxable income—and not because the money they get is obtained legally. Which is why crime didn't go up around here when the club moved in. If anything, it went down."

"If you don't call *murder* crime," she mutters.

"Are you wanting me to throw hot oatmeal in your face?"

She grabs her coffee mug and begins to pour sugar into the empty container. "People are scared, Tessa. Since the club moved in, things around here *have* changed, and now we have murders? Some men are talking about banding together to run the Leidolf out of town and honestly, I can't blame them. I don't see why Gary and them stay in this one-traffic-light town anyway. It doesn't make any sense."

I listen to the sound of bikes outside. Chopper is leaving and Zeno is taking his place. And I know exactly why these men made Hinton their home. A town like this gets in your blood, making it thick as glue at the county line. You might leave, but you always come back. Everywhere else smothers you. Stiffens you up until you have to come back to the air and dirt of the river. Gary knows this better than any of us, and the rest of the guys have the river flowing through them now, too.

I take my hot bowl from the microwave and sit at the table. "The *man* wanting to run the Leidolf off better understand he isn't intimidating. We don't fear him and we certainly don't revere him. So let your dad know the easily intimidated people that he gets to control for no other reason than he's related to them, are a band of merry idiots he's going to get hurt if he messes with the club."

She pours her coffee and replaces the pot with a thud. "I didn't say it was *our* dad. I said *people*, Tessa. And like it or not, he's your dad, too."

"He's a worthless wanna-be and I'm neither a child nor weak-minded. I see him for what he is and it would serve you to do the same."

My family is part of the *blood is thicker than water* clan, a bit that gets old fast when the men whose backs you're supposed to have beat their wives and children because it makes them feel strong. Proof of how weak my dad is lies in the fact that Gary doesn't have to tell him not to show up in the bar, Dad hasn't ever attempted to step foot on Leidolf ground. Unlike the handful of times he's presumed to show up on my doorstep. I came home once to find Beth had let him inside. That didn't end well.

"You're supposed to be staying with Arnold," I tell her between mouthfuls of oatmeal.

She shrugs. "He snores. And how did you know I wasn't there anyway?"

I scrape my spoon over the bottom of the bowl. "The guys are surveilling the house."

Her body goes rigid and ever so slowly she turns to face me, eyes wide and lips pressed into a hard line. I slide my bowl away. I wish I hadn't gotten so drunk that I spilled the beans about all the murders to her, but I did. And she needs to take the threat seriously. "I'm going to put an announcement in the paper. Women need to be vigilant, and all of us deserve to know we're being hunted."

Her lips part and she takes a breath, making me realize she's been holding it. "I agree, and it's why I don't want to be followed around by a bunch of men who are probably hiding the culprit."

"I didn't say they were following you. They don't like you, remember?" I make a face to match the one she's giving me. "They're watching *my* house. If you don't like it, you can go stay with Arnold."

She folds her arms. "Ever heard about the wolf in sheep's clothing? Their club name literally means *wolf.*"

I get up from the table and plop my bowl into the sink. "They are *descendants* of the wolf. Protectors. And I better not hear a single whisper about you running around talking badly about my boys." I face her. "There are lines you can't cross, and accusing innocent men of being butchers is one of them. Don't let me hear you say it again."

"Fine." She slams a lid on her to-go cup. "Chief is going to be hotter than a hornet when he hears about your little newspaper warning, but I'm glad you're finally doing something other than tucking yourself into a *safe place* while the rest of us are out here being forced from our homes and fighting for our lives!"

"This isn't your house, it's mine. And you could have just as easily gone to the paper yourself instead of running down to the post office to spread gossip with Marla."

She lifts her chin and sets her jaw. "I don't get to run around like the rules don't apply to me. If I go against the Chief, this town will flay me in the churchyard. But *you* they'll immortalize as a saint. So go run and warn everyone, Tessa, because it isn't gossip when it comes from you." She heads toward the front door, a stomp in her step. "I'll go tell Marla we're not allowed to talk, that *you're* the only one who can warn people."

~13~

After my fight with Beth, I shower and have Zeno drive me to the newspaper office. Before we make it to the bar, Chief is lighting up my phone. Sally Jane called him right after she took the announcement I submitted. She's always been a suck-up so I expected no less and therefore ignore Chief's calls.

Shortly after I make it into my office, I'm summoned to the front where a purple-faced Chief is waiting. He says the newspaper announcement isn't going to run and that's okay with me. I have a new plan. "You and Mayor are welcome at the town hall we're hosting in the bar tonight."

He jabs a finger at me. "I told you my suspicions in confidence so you would look after yourself better. Not so you could go spreading rumors because if anyone around here is in danger, it's *you*, running around here all hours of the day and night on the back of whatever your cousin dragged in last."

I grin at the Leidolf, who are paying close attention to the Chief's hostility yet giving the man some leniency. "Chopper's a little shady but the rest don't even try to feel me up when I'm kissing them goodnight. What kind of bad boys are those?"

Chief slams a hand on the bar. "Dang you, Tessa! This isn't a joke. You're going to get yourself or someone else hurt!"

Randy places a hand on Chief's shoulder. A warning. I wave him away and round the bar, slipping my own hand onto Chief's elbow and leading him out the front door. "Anyone ever told you not to walk into a viper den and rile them up?"

He shrugs me off his arm with a huff. "Anyone ever told you that I've got enough of a mess on my hands without you stirring things up with this town hall? You don't even have the authority to call a town hall meeting!"

I look over his shoulder to where a couple of the kitchen staff are unloading supplies from a van. If anyone feels like ordering food tonight, we want to be prepared. "You see, that's the thing. I didn't ask for permission, and the townspeople already RSVPing to the social media event page I set up is all the authority I need." I smile at him. "You're more than welcome to come say your piece, and Mayor, too. We were kind of hoping both of you would be here to address the people who elected you."

"I wasn't elected, I was appointed. And what exactly do you want me to say?" he spits. "You want me to go into the gory details? You want me to unleash on all these people what my men are devastated from seeing?"

"I want your *elected by the mayor* self to explain to your people that we have a *killer* running loose around us. Let them know your theories, tell them to be vigilant, and give us any clues that might lead someone to help you catch this guy."

His jaw works, eyes hard. "I wish I would have never told you about the others."

"Well, you did," I chide. "And it doesn't seem fair that I should be the only woman warned to be extra vigilant, though I appreciate the soft spot you have for me."

He bristles at my sarcasm. "I only warned you because of the company you keep."

I lean toward him. "If you're so scared of the Leidolf, then why do you come in here and give them your hard-earned upstanding citizen money?"

He turns on his heel and storms toward his car. "Chief!" I call after him. "If you think it's one of them mutilating women, come to the meeting and stare each of them in the face. See who flinches first!"

Gary is waiting for me inside the door, arms folded over his barrel chest. I shrug. "Chief has to yell sometimes. It relieves his blood pressure."

"Sounded to me like you were the one doing the yelling."

I shrug again. "He couldn't hear me over his own shouting."

Gary drops his arms and sighs. "I *know* Chief has a soft spot for you, most of the town does, but you've got to leave this alone. We'll have your town hall, and then you're not going to get into screaming matches with the chief of police in front of the bar anymore. Got it?"

I've never really felt the love from many townsfolk, and the only reason Chief treats me special is because of a certain four-year-old boy. Erin never told anyone who the father was and when she worked here, everyone gossiped that she wasn't telling because she didn't know which Leidolf member knocked her up. But the night I stumbled across Chief's cruiser out by the dump, Erin was serving him the kind of cocktail that leads to babies. Now she lives over in MacArthur doing telemarketing, and I imagine Chief had a hand in her relocation because that boy is the spitting image of him. One he doesn't need seen in the town where his wife and two other daddy-look-alike sons live. "I'll do my best, Gary. But sometimes you men *need* a woman to yell at you."

~

Erin was an adult when I was fourteen and first stumbled upon her and Chief, but she was *barely* an adult. I always wondered if they kept seeing each other and her later pregnancy confirmed they did. What her pregnancy didn't tell me was if Chief might be taking others for a ride on a hot summer night. I never saw him with anyone else and nighttime was my favorite part of the day. I'd roam all over the town, trek through the woods and go for a midnight swim. No matter where I went, Warren always found me. And I wanted nothing more than to spend my life having those kinds of nights.

Being part of Riverside Grille gives me a nightlife without me having to roam through the darkness on my own. And I *would* be on my own now, because there's no more Warren to stalk me through the woods. No more Warren hiding just under the water's surface so he can grab me and drag me out into the river where he can kiss me under the stars. All those nights I wasted on him, thinking my future was out there in his arms when all along the place I belonged just hadn't rode into town yet. As much as I regret every second I spent with Warren, I'm glad Gary was back when my dreamworld exploded. Without him, and without Chopper, I wouldn't have survived the heartbreak. I did though, and I'm going to survive this serial killer. So is every other woman in this town.

People start arriving at the bar just after five even though the meeting is set for seven. Women with children left their kids with husbands, boyfriends or grandpas and started trickling in as soon as their childcare was provided for. The women who can't make it have called to ask that they be kept in the loop. Due to the Leidolf rules, there's no recording allowed in the Grille, so Gary said no, even though I did ask for an exception. He said Beth could take handwritten notes and share them, a task he's giving her in hopes that the official job will persuade her to report actual facts instead of gossip. I just hope she doesn't decide to pull out a cellphone and attempt an audio recording. The guys are good at sniffing out things like that, and they'll smash her phone before she can blink three times in a row.

"Tess," Gary's voice is measured with sorrow. "Chopper's staying out here with you but I'm taking the others into the sanctuary for a few minutes. If Beth shows up, make sure she understands her place. The Leidolf are *not* participants in this meeting. Our words and actions don't need to be repeated."

"I understand." I place a hand along his jaw. "Thank you for letting me do this here."

He presses his lips to my forehead. "Stay where Chopper can see you."

~14~

Gary and the other Leidolf members fan out around the Grille. None of them are interacting with anyone. They're statues. Watchmen. Hunters. And I know they have their reasons, and me bringing this many people into the bar at once is not only an invasion of their home but puts them at a severe disadvantage as far as sheer numbers are concerned, but the women in this room are *not* enemies. And they're not prey. So the stone-cut faces of the club are grating on my already frazzled nerves.

"Can you guys tone down the assassin vibe?" I whisper from beside Gary's shoulder. He doesn't respond. "Great," I mutter. "If our esteemed mayor or dignified chief don't show up, I was hoping you'd step in?"

"You're the one who called this meeting."

I slump against the wall. "Yeah, but I'm not a public speaker, and you keep telling me to stay away from this whole murder situation so…"

He looks down at me. "Sounds like you need to go prepare a speech."

I walk away from him, looking over the amassing crowd once more. It doesn't only consist of women. Men are peppered throughout, everyone in this room equally as terrified as the next person. I severely underestimated the level of unease already existing in town and from the way they're looking at me like I have some magical answer that will wipe away all their fears, I

58

can only hope Chief shows up. Or that the next person through the door brings tidings of an arrest.

I glance to the entrance and spot Beth coming in with her hand tucked into Arnold's. I make eye contact with her and she mouths "I'm sorry."

I cross the room and open my arms, hugging her tight. "I'm sorry, too. I've been snappy lately, taking all my fears and anxieties out on you."

She runs her fingers through my hair, straightening the strands like a big sister is apt to do. "I know you're under a lot of stress. I imagine Gary is torn up, and that's tearing you up." I nod and she frowns. "Any word yet on when Samantha's body is going to be released?"

I shake my head. "We're hoping the medical examiner will be finished soon so we can lay her to rest, but no word on when that's going to happen as of yet."

She takes in the buzzing room. "You amassed a crowd on short notice. I should have been here to help. Anything I can do now?"

"Gary said you can take notes. He'll have to approve them, but we'll post them in the social media group I set up once he does. Go get a pen and pad from my office because you know the rules—no audio. Or video."

Her eyes are patronizing but she nods. I place a hand on her shoulder. "Take good notes. Maybe what happens here tonight will result in someone coming forward with information."

Her nose crinkles. "You don't think they would have already?"

Arnold slips his hand from hers and rests his palm against her back. "We were talking… Do you think Samantha might have met this person somewhere and invited them to town?"

Beth looks up at him and then back at me. "He's saying if she was out buying drugs, and you know, met some dealer and had them bring her some pills here."

"We've considered that angle." I look past them to where Sally Jane just waltzed in and is making her way right to the front of the bar. "You two go get what you need and settle in somewhere. We plan to start right at seven."

Heading for Sally Jane's perch, which just happens to be near where I plan to stand when I start this meeting fifteen minutes from now, I maneuver into her line of sight and give her a polite smile. "Hello, Sally Jane."

"Hi, Tessa," she mutters, averting her eyes and scribbling unnecessarily on her notepad.

A commotion kicks up behind us in the packed room. I turn just as Mayor Smith walks through the door, Chief beside him and two deputies behind him. There's also a camera crew and what looks to be a real-life reporter. I glance at Sally Jane. She's shooting daggers at the newcomer. "Friend of yours?"

"That's a reporter from two counties over, they think they're big-time just because they have a larger population."

I nudge her. "If you didn't rat us out, you'd be getting the exclusive."

Her shoulders lift, eyes still fixed on the door. "Huh, would you look at that. It's been a while since Warren's been on this side of town. Rumor has it, he's real selective about who he keeps company with these days."

There's a full second when I almost laugh, but then her smug eyes turn to mine and I know it's true. Warren is in the bar. I give her back a nice hard pat. "Sally Jane, why don't you go on and venture out of here to where it's less safe? Maybe play in the street or hitch a ride with a serial killer."

Feet feeling like they're stuck in cement, I let my fury push them forward, toward a figure I haven't set eyes on in years. Warren is skulking along the front wall, past the row of one-way windows. His head turns and the stubble along his jaw makes my heart do those little hiccups it started doing when I was thirteen and he kissed me for the first time. I'd just shoved a spider down the back of his shirt and when he caught me, he held me against him with one hand and tugged my mouth to his with the other.

Teeth grinding, I block his path. "Walk back out the way you came or I'll have the Leidolf carry you out piece by pathetic piece."

He doesn't make eye contact, scanning the crowd around us as if I'm not about to explode. "This is a public meeting. I have as much of a right to be here as anyone else."

"You're a man, so you have a zero percent chance of being killed by this murderer but a one hundred percent chance of dying if you don't get out of my sight right now."

He breaks and looks, eyes slamming into mine. "I have a mom, sisters, and all kinds of women I care about spread all over this state, so I'm staying."

Heat rises through my body, and not because he excites me anymore. "Get. Out."

"Darn it, Tessa!" He runs a hand through his hair. "When are you going to get over this childish grudge?"

"When you're dead," I growl.

My words hang thick between us. His chest heaves, anger rushing through him the same as me. I know it because I know him as well as I know my own flesh.

"Warren!" Marcie's shrill voice breaks the heat of his glare. He turns to look for her face in the crowd.

My words come out in a rumbled snarl. "Take your girlfriend and get out of this bar."

His head snaps back around. "Jealousy isn't pretty on you."

I step into him, bumping him off-kilter with the unexpected contact. He takes a step back. I advance. This time he doesn't move. I stretch myself into his face. "There's not a bit of jealousy in me. All I feel for Marcie is pity. I only have one sister, she has *two*." His throat works, an attempt to swallow the unease of my words. My lips tug up over my teeth. "That's right, Warren. I know you screwed my sister. Beth told me *everything*."

His eyes narrow. "Your sister is a compulsive liar. Not to mention a b—" My palm across his face shuts him up, and hushes the crowd. Blood draws to the corner of his mouth. He wipes it and stares at his fingers.

"Get. Out," I order, heart beating once, twice, and then he's gone, busting out the front door with Marcie on his heels.

~15~

Warren used to say my brain was a Ferrari while everyone else was driving Volvos. But Warren never liked anyone that much, especially Beth. So when it came to people picking out all the differences between her and me, Warren skewed heavily in my favor. Especially if doing so demoralized my sister. I always defended her to him but as it turns out, he was only picking on her because he liked her. Because he wanted her and not me. All those years of me watching her back when what I should have been doing was watching my own.

At least I don't have to worry about public speaking tonight. I've done enough by way of public displays so it was a relief when Mayor took my spot behind the bar and began to relay information to the gathered men and women. The details he and Chief are giving aren't as vague as I'd hoped, though. Chief brought notes from the autopsies of the older murders. All four females were beaten badly before they died. And they didn't die until *after* they were cut open. "You mean…" Beth's voice trails off, her eyes not the only ones in the room wet with tears. "He's cutting them up when they're still able to feel it?"

Chief's voice is soft. Despite his extramarital affairs that say otherwise, I've known him to be a genuinely caring man. "At this stage in the investigation, we're unclear on how alert the women may have been. All we can tell you is what I've already disclosed." His eyes lift to where I'm sitting in the back of the room, shaken by his words and the altercation with Warren. Chopper is on my left and Gary on my right. "A lot of you have been calling the station and we're happy to take reports on any leads you think you might have. But the more bogged down we are listening to you think the postman looked at you sideways, the less time we have for the investigation."

I get his message. I created more work for him, and I don't even have to notice his glance in Gena's direction to know she's called and reported her nephews. A leaf could fall off a tree and she'd accuse one of those sweet boys of stealing it. Two sets of twins, and for some reason she got it in her head that her brother's spawn are unnatural.

Standing so my voice can be heard above the buzz of loud whispers, I address part of Chief's concerns. "If you need volunteers to answer phones, we can arrange that. I'm even happy to let people call in here with leads." His narrowed eyes tell me he's getting *my* message. The offer I just made will spread and if the people think the Leidolf are more capable of finding the murderer than he is, they'll call us. It's a power play, one I know Gary would approve had I asked him, but most importantly, my offer is real. Despite being told to stay out of things, I want to help find the killer.

Mayor holds up his hands, stopping the shouts of others who are all eager to get involved. "We appreciate the outpouring of support. It's what makes our town the wonderful place to live that we all love so much. Rest assured that we're doing everything within our power to find the person responsible and bring them to justice. In the meantime, what's most helpful is for everyone to remain calm." He waves his hands again as the crowd murmurs about the impossibility of remaining anything remotely close to calm. "I know, I know. I might as well ask you to thread a camel through a needle's eye. Just be careful, pay attention to your surroundings, and don't talk to strangers."

I roll my eyes. "Yeah, ladies, let's *us* stay away from the serial killers. I'm sure they all wear badges to identify themselves, so it should be easy to avoid them."

Chief frowns. "What he's saying is be vigilant. Not so afraid that we call and report a rafter who happened to take a break on our banks when he floated down the river, but vigilant enough to report a man on the riverbank who doesn't have a pole and who isn't dressed for water activities. We need good leads, not those born of fear."

Gary places a hand on my shoulder before I can open my mouth again and breaks his silence. "This town means a lot to us. Tessa and I were born and raised here, and it's where I brought my brothers home." He acknowledges the Leidolf around us. "We're here to help. If any woman ever feels threatened and she sees one of my brothers, I give my word that she can trust them to protect her. We'll be making patrols, so you'll be seeing us in your neighborhoods."

Chief's jaw works and I realize Gary did a much better job with his power play. He just circumvented the entire purpose of the police force. He's telling the people that if they want to be safe, they should rely on the Leidolf.

~

It's late and the bar hasn't wound down. People are too afraid or too happy to have something to gossip about to go home. I slip out the back and into my vehicle, sitting in the silence of the Highlander with Randy and Rick watching me. I lean the seat back and stare at the sky through the moonroof. The club has never really been at odds with the police in this town. For the most part, we all get along and Chief always makes a point of stopping in to say hello even if he isn't doing any drinking. A few times he's even brought his family in for a meal. Tonight felt like we severed those ties. Whatever information Gary was given access to when we went in to give our *statements* might very well be the last bit of information Chief decides to share with us.

Sitting up, I put one foot on the brake and hover my other foot over the gas. Randy is facing away from me but Zeno is watching. I start my engine and throw the vehicle into gear, glad I parked facing out of the space because if I had to back up, I would never make it out of this lot alone.

Zeno gets a hand on my rear passenger door but it's locked. I hit the gas, glancing through the rearview at the end of the alley just before I peel onto the street. Randy's on his phone. I'm sure he's talking to Gary but there's someplace I need to go, and I'm going there alone.

I drive to the patch of river where Samantha's body was found and park along the roadside. Crime scene tape flaps in the breeze in front of the path that leads over the embankment. This is where I was the day I found Samantha's necklace. The one she always wore as a teen, a gold chain with a diamond-encrusted unicorn pendant. All fake, of course. But fancy to a seventh-grader like me. I'd found that chain buried in the sand underneath a log I'd sat on to watch the older kids swimming in the river. I knew where they were because Beth had snuck out of the house to go with them. I followed her. She yelled at me, though, so I didn't swim, just sat and watched them splashing in the water until that old log rolled and I found myself with a skinned knee and a sprained wrist. Samantha took one look at me and chained that necklace she didn't know she'd lost around my neck.

How bizarre that *this* is where she'd take her last breath all these years later. If, in fact, this *is* where she was murdered. From the road, the beach below is hidden. And from up here on top, the hillside looks too steep and dense to reach the river. But if you know just where to go, the old path will take you to one of the nicest holes along this stretch of river. Most of the time it's claimed by teenagers in town, generations of us having had some of our first kisses here. But whether you're young or old, to know where this path is, you *have* to be a local.

Contemplating whether or not an outsider could stumble upon this trail, or the possibility of someone floating along the river happening upon the seemingly secluded beach and learning its secret path, I duck under the tape and make my way along the trail, using my phone for light. I pick my way to the beach and shine my light along the river's edge, looking for the drop-off where I imagine Sam was floating when Duncan hooked her.

"Tessa!" My name slices through the darkness behind me. I shine my phone back toward the head of the trail, remaining silent. "It's Matt." He holds his own phone up to his face, lighting himself in an unflattering glow. "Are you okay? What are you doing down there?"

"How did you know I was here?"

"I followed you." He ducks under the tape, shining his light down the hill. "Are you…is this where…is there blood down there?"

"Doubt it. It rained pretty hard last night." I click my phone light off. "Why are you following me?"

Silence builds in the night. He clicks his phone light off. "This will be easier to say in the dark."

"So say it then."

He clears his throat. "I have the hots for you. Like, dream-of-you-every-night and see-you-every-time-I-blink kind of hots. So, I was at the dollar store and saw your car go by, and I know you don't live in this direction, and there was that guy you slapped tonight…"

"You followed me to see if me slapping him was foreplay?"

He laughs. "Yep. And before you say men are stupid, let me remind you that I'm not the one standing in a murder scene right now."

"Are you a murderer?"

"In the serial killer handbook, rule number two is *Don't tell anyone you're a serial killer.*

I grin. "What's rule number one?"

He turns his phone light back on. "Follow the girl you like."

I turn my light on and head for the path. "Get your best pick-up line ready, I'm coming up."

When I reach the road, Matt is leaning against his car, a bottle of vodka in his hand. "I lied. Nothing against the Grille, but I was suffocating after that meeting, and I couldn't afford to stay there and buy all the drinks I'm going to need tonight."

"So you were buying alcohol when you saw me pass by?"

He nods. "You being here makes me think you need this bottle as much as I do. Want to help me drink it?"

I walk toward him. "Here?"

He steps forward, close enough that only the bottle is between us. "My place. Or yours. I'm flexible."

I wrap my hand above his on the bottle. "You might need to prove that to me."

{~16~}

~ 16 ~

It's been a while since I've had the kind of hangover that makes me unable to get out of bed. Even longer since I've woken up in an unfamiliar bed. I pull Matt's pillow over my head. "What time is it?"

"Ten." His voice sounds like a smile. My body tingles. I'm not so hungover I don't remember his lips all over me last night. "Want some coffee?"

I peek out from under the pillow. "How are you functioning right now? And how do you look so good?"

"Same way you look good enough to eat. Again." His hand slips underneath the covers. "Before you go, there's one more dream I want to tell you about."

This is how last night started. Three shots in, he relaxed enough to tell me he dreamed about the feel of my lips. After we kissed, we did more shots and he said he dreamed about the taste of my neck. And about what I'd feel like underneath him. One dream after another, we acted them out, satisfying ourselves with flesh and alcohol until we forgot all about the murders. This man is a master of his own body and last night, he owned mine.

"You have the best dreams, but I have to go." I climb over him, the only way out of this ridiculously small bed. "Now that you've found your tongue and used it, maybe you'll manage to find my number."

~

69

When I got back to the bar last night, I parked in the front and gave Dillon a wave before disappearing into Matt's building. He would let Gary know where I was and call back any members who had gone out to look for me. I worried Gary or Chopper would break down Matt's door but they didn't, and after those first few shots, I forgot all about them.

"Where do you think you're going?" Randy is leaning on my Highlander's driver's door.

"Home." I sigh. "My head is pounding so I'm not going inside the noisy Grille."

"The lunch crowd hasn't got here yet." He nods to his bike. It's parked behind my vehicle. "But I'll take you home, darlin'. Because I don't think you want to answer to Gary until you've had time to sober all the way up."

I stomp to his bike and slide onto the seat. I don't feel like driving anyway, and the more I think about the nerve Warren had to walk into the bar last night, the angrier I become. It's Gary's conversations with him that gave Warren the courage. So my cousin might be annoyed with me, but I have my own bones to pick with him. Once I get some sleep.

Without forcing any more conversation, Randy drops me at my house and walks around the property while I go inside. I was hoping to have the place to myself, at least until Beth got home from work, but not long after I fell into bed and got comfortable did she come tiptoeing into my room, the squeaky board three feet from my threshold giving her away. I pop an eye open. "You don't have to sneak, I'm awake."

"Are you sick?" she questions, not used to me being home through the day.

"No." I yawn. "Just tired."

She sits beside me, scooting over until she's resting against my legs. "Tell me about it. There was no way I was coming back here by myself after that meeting last night, so I stayed at *Snoring Arnold's*." Her eyes bore into the one of mine I've managed to keep open. "Did you know? About how the women were beaten and…cut?"

I rest a forearm over my eyes, the visions of Samantha and Layla too much to handle. "I didn't know all of what Chief reported last night, but he'd told me some of it."

Her swallow echoes through our silence. "Layla was beheaded, and the others weren't. So what does that mean? Two killers are out there?"

I move my arm and open it wide for her. She slides down in the bed and curls against my side. I press my lips to her temple. "Whatever Chief is seeing in the case files, he's convinced the same person is responsible for all five, so let's not add more, okay?"

"It just doesn't make sense," she whispers. "Last night he said the third victim was asphyxiated, and only three of the four who still had their heads showed signs of head trauma. How can it be the same killer? Don't those guys have a signature or something? A pattern?"

I smooth my fingers over her hair, offering what little comfort I have to give. "I guess Chief is looking at the actual cause of death being the filleting, not the other things. So he's linking them that way."

"So…" she sniffs, "they're almost killed, and then resuscitated or something?"

I knead my fingers along the tense muscles of her neck. "It sounds like the monster gets off on watching them bleed out, so yeah, I guess maybe he's doing it like you say."

Typically, the front door opening wouldn't scare me, but the blanket of trust I've had surrounding the people in this town is gone. I sit up and slip away from Beth, gently sliding open my nightstand drawer and retrieving the pistol. I press a finger to my lips, silencing Beth. "Where are the wolves?" she mouths.

I don't answer her. It could be one of the club members in the living room, but I'm not taking any chances. I slink toward the bedroom door, eyes trained on the hallway. "Tessa!" Mom's voice rings out from the location of the kitchen. Beth and I both sigh.

Straightening, I move back to my nightstand and put the pistol away. Beth swings her feet off the side of the mattress. "I think we should have a new rule. No convicts in the house."

I frown at her. "Mom's only been to jail because she covers for Dad."

If it weren't for the despicable man she married, Mom could have been something. She sings like a canary and in her day, she was known as a true beauty. Instead of cashing in on either of those, she married a man who beats and berates her, one she defends even though he uses her as a pawn on top of everything else. It's never *his* name on the bad checks, only hers. He's just the one beating her until she writes the check they both know will bounce.

Mom makes it to the bedroom door and leans against the frame, leveling a glare at me. I lift my hands in a guessing gesture. "No black eyes, so I assume you're not here to ask if you can move in?"

"Don't sass your daddy like that," she snaps, her full lips pressing together and her thick dark hair shaking. She's had this twitch for as long as I can remember. A few of her sisters do, too. So it isn't brain damage from being hit too often.

"If your husband were here, I'd sass him to his face. Instead, you're here, hollering like your pony is stuck in a fence, and doing it without a nod to the hangover I have. That means today, all my sass is just for you, Mom."

"You wouldn't have a hangover if you'd stay away from that boy," she spits, eyes narrowing. Even angry, she's still beautiful, though hard years of life have tried their best to wrangle that loveliness away from her. She waves her hand toward nothing in particular. "I told you he's trouble! But there you go laying with him again, throwing everything away so he can knock you up and leave you with a houseful of mouths to feed!"

I look over my shoulder and Beth mouths *"Warren"*. I face Mom, wondering if it was Beth who told her I was with him last night. It wouldn't surprise me to hear she turned me slapping him across the face into something she felt was juicier, hoping word wouldn't get back to me. I think she spreads lies about me because she knows even if I do hear the rumors she starts, I won't call her out on them. But I don't only because she *has* to know people around here talk to me. This means her lies aren't really about me; they're about her need to feel important. And I have thicker skin than most. Rumors aren't going to tear me down.

Letting Beth have whatever power she attributes to being the one to always have something to say about someone else, I just stare at Mom, waiting for whatever she's going to throw out next. When I went through puberty and became what some people think is beautiful, she'd brush my hair at night and tell me I was going to be her meal ticket. In those days, if I could have helped her in some way, I would have. But every time she said she was going to leave her lousy husband, it ended up being a lie. Now she doesn't even attempt to pretend she's going to leave him. This woman is going to die staring into that man's face and there's not a thing this *meal ticket* can do about it.

Mom's arms cross. "I heard about you and Warren causing a scene at the bar. Don't think anyone is fooled by the two of you. He probably told you to slap him so Gary wouldn't suspect anything. Conniving little punk."

"Those are strong words." I mock her posture. "Gary would be mighty upset if he knew you were calling him a punk."

"You know good and well who I'm talking about!" She yanks her arms free of her body and thrusts them into the air. Behind her, Matt is standing just outside the screen door, flowers in hand and eyes fixed on us. I give him a smile. He smiles back. Mom turns around, face going pale.

I wave Matt inside. "Don't mind us, Mom is just telling me the boy I was with last night is nothing but trouble. What do you think? Are you worth all this fighting?"

~17~

The lobes of Matt's ears are red as he steps inside the house. I pad over the old hardwood planks and accept the flowers he's offering, peeking at Mom over the blooms. She won't say much now that company is in the room. Neither will Beth. They tend to lose their tongues when people outside the family are around.

He looks at my mom. "I don't want to upset you, ma'am. I just came to check on Tessa. We had a…late night."

"Late night, and an early morning." I correct. That redness climbs over his neck and into his cheeks.

Mom steps forward with a grin, her tone sweeter than honey out of the comb. "It's alright. Just as long as she's okay, that's all we care about."

His eyes crinkle as he smiles at me. "With a killer running around, I'd say you are worried about her. I doubt she'd go traipsing off alone in the dark, though. She's too smart for that."

I set his flowers on the card table that's next to the door. "There are a lot of things I'm dumb enough to do once. It's getting me to do them twice that's the problem."

"That's good to know." He nods toward the door. "Can we talk?"

After last night, I wouldn't expect Matt to be shy, but as we leave the house he breaks eye contact, looking between me and the old white sedan my mom parked halfway on the sidewalk. "Uh-oh, are you breaking up with me?" I tease. His throat bobs.

"I'm just kidding. Last night was fun, and this morning, but there aren't any strings."

"I…um…" he stammers, glancing over his shoulder in time to catch the curtain Mom and Beth are hiding behind flutter back into place. "I had fun last night, too. More this morning when we were both sober."

I lead him down the steps to the street so I can hop up onto Mom's hood. Normally she'd yell at me for this, but with Matt here, she won't say a word. "Sober is always better."

His blue eyes glint, the darker band around his irises drawing my attention. "So we could do that again?"

"Do what? Stay sober?"

He scrubs his face. "I mean, can we go on a date? I'll cook or take you out someplace nice. Whatever you want to do. I just want to spend time with you."

As much as people compliment me, very few men ever bother to ask me out and even fewer bring me flowers. "I have to go to the Grille tonight, but we can do something tomorrow."

A smile splits his face. "Should I pick you up here?"

I slide off the hood. "Sure."

His fingers glide along my wrist. "How about I make you dinner? I already picked up what I need from the grocery store, I just need to borrow your kitchen."

I smile. "Sounds like you're a presumptuous man."

His hand moves up my arm, eyes igniting. "I know what I want. All that's left is figuring out what you want, and giving it to you."

I glance down the street to where Dillon fires up his bike and wonder if Matt would have stopped if Dillon had been parked directly in front of the house. I meet Matt's passionate eyes. "What I want right now is a shower, but you're not ready to take that step with me yet." I kiss his cheek. "You can borrow my kitchen. Just make enough for three because my sister will probably be here."

Dillon drops me at the Grille but Gary isn't around. He's off with Chopper *questioning* someone about Samantha's murder. I was excited until Brian told me the person wasn't a suspect, just someone they thought had information. Information regarding Gary's theory that Sam's murder was an attack against him and the club.

I reach out to Chief to see if he has anything new to report but as I suspected, that bridge was burned. I'm hoping it's only singed, though, because he took one full breath before hanging up on me the last time I called.

Chief doesn't seem to be the only toasty man around me. The Leidolf aren't as chatty today and I can't figure out if it's because I got by them last night or because they're laser-focused on their hunt.

One man isn't icing me out, though. I sit in my office and scroll through Matt's messages. His first text let me know he *does* have my number. His second said he can't stop thinking about me. But it's the third that makes me feel like he isn't only here until the newness of us wears off. His words don't make me feel like a fading interest, an object to pass his time until someone else comes along. *You have a way of tying my tongue, some kind of voodoo I haven't been able to get past. But you're the first thing I saw when I moved to town two years ago, and the instant the landlord told me you work in the bar next to my building, I signed the lease right then and there. You've been the bright spot in all my days, Tessa. And I finally get to tell you.*

Matt's been a bright spot for me, too. One of those guys who make you smile because of how nervous they get when you're around. I wasn't sure his backwardness was only because of me, though. I've never been the only female around when I've flirted with him, making tiny beads of sweat sprout along his brow. Sometimes I even thought maybe he wasn't staring at me but at one of the other bartenders. Now I know he was pining for me, and his attention couldn't have come at a better time. I need a distraction from the heaviness of these murders, and if anything is to be learned in the aftermath of what these women went through, it's that life is moment to moment. I intend to soak up every good minute I can.

It's getting late and Gary and Chopper still aren't back. I texted Gary but he isn't responding. So I text Matt. *Can I come over?*

Anytime, he responds. A smile breaks across my face. I slip out the Grille's back door and tell Zeno goodnight, giving him a wink before disappearing behind the thick mass of rhododendrons that separates our back lot from Matt's building. It's a tight fit but when Gary bought the bar, we checked out the neighborhood, and I remember the pad of concrete just behind the back corner of Matt's building, where his back door opens to nothing but a wall of yet more rhododendrons. For fire safety, the building has to have a back exit. Now it can be my own personal door.

From the amount of leaves and debris covering the concrete pad, Matt hasn't ever opened this door before. I beat on the steel slab. He finally opens the door, wearing boxers and a confused look. I grin. "I took a shortcut."

He reaches for my hand and pulls me against his broad chest. "I knew renting this building would be perfect."

~18~

It's nice falling asleep in Matt's arms. And waking up in them. He gives my butterflies *butterflies*, and makes all the time I've waited just to have him talk to me worth it. I snuggle against him. "You're right, this building was a great idea."

He runs a strand of my hair through his fingertips. "Will you stay here again tonight?"

I run my foot along his, the two of us tucked into the sheets of his full-size bed, my head on his chest and my belly so absolutely satisfied. "We'll fit better in my queen bed, but we've been fairly noisy and I have a roommate."

His hand tightens on my waist. "Maybe we should find a place of our own."

I look up at him. "Are you asking me to move in with you?"

He smiles. "I don't expect you to move in here, but we could rent a house."

"I already have a house."

He readjusts me so I'm on my back and he's perched overtop, gazing down into my eyes. "You have a house, but *we* don't have a house. I'm not saying we should outright buy one, that wouldn't make sense this early on. But you're... I think you might be the one for me, Tessa. And with..." He looks away and I cup my hands along his face, pulling his gaze back to mine.

"And what, Matt?"

He swallows. "I was dragging my feet. Then a woman died. Someone you knew. Someone I saw in the bar a few times when I came in for lunch."

"And you're scared I'll be next, so you're making your move? So you can have me until I get murdered?"

He curls a hand around the back of my neck and pulls my lips to his. "I made a move because I'm scared, because I want to keep you safe, and because I'm jealous. When you slapped that guy, whatever the reason, it came from a place of passion and I want all of your passion, Tessa. Whatever you have to give, I want it."

I let him guide my mouth, finally feeling like someone wants all of me. Like someone *sees* me, and they don't want to change me or weed out the parts that don't suit them. Matt's been watching me long enough to know who I am, and he likes it well enough to want to move in with me. Outside of Beth, no one has ever wanted to live with me before.

I have a closet in Gary's apartment so when I stay at the bar I have clothes and toiletries, but I don't keep any of my things in Chopper's apartment and he's never offered to let me. Because the feelings we have for each other are a different kind of love. More of a fondness, really. And Chopper's the only man I've gone all the way with since Warren destroyed me.

I slide my hands down Matt's back. "I'm going to go check on things next door, then I'm going to come back, and we're going to pick up right here. Don't bother getting dressed."

He smiles. "I'll put a closed sign in the front window and wait for you right here."

~

"Where's Gary?" I ask Chopper. He's standing by the Grille's back door, staring at Matt's building.

He breaks his stare and opens the door for me. "Cheryl's here."

"Cool." I head into the hallway. He follows me. "Leave Matt alone. Or I won't leave any of the women in this town alone, and we'll see how *you* like being cut off."

"It's not a good time for you to start up with him."

"Bite me, Chopper."

"Gladly."

I flip him off and grin when I hear his chuckle. It's so rare to get those sounds out of him, and they're melodious when he manages to let himself smile. Another person who can carry a tune is my little cousin Cheryl. She's seventeen and has been singing all her life, hitting notes that are rare even for the most professionally trained singer. I walk up behind Gary and slide my hand over his shoulder while Cheryl plays her guitar and practices a song for Samantha's funeral. "It's beautiful."

Gary nods. "Sam always did love to hear Cheryl sing." He turns his neck, looking up at me. "You're spending a lot of time with Matt."

"Despite everything that's going on, he's managing to make me happy."

He drags my hand from his shoulder and grips it tightly in his. "That's all I've ever wanted for you, Tessa. For you to find happiness in this world."

He doesn't say *before it's too late*, but I see the sentiment in his eyes. Without Samantha, there's a joy he'll never feel again. I don't understand his loss completely because Warren is still alive, but the pain of him ripping my still-beating heart from my chest is as vivid as the image of what was done to Gary's Samantha.

I wrap my arms around Gary, the two of us turning our attention back to Cheryl's cherub face. "We're going to make the people who hurt us pay for their actions."

His chest rises and falls. "My brothers and I will make them pay."

"Me, too. I want to be there when you put a stake through their heart."

"No." His voice rumbles through me. "You're *are* going to do as you're told. And you're going to stay where I tell you to stay. Here. Your house." His jaw ticks. "Next door. Places where I have eyes on you." He pierces me with a hard stare. "Don't you *ever* attempt to dodge my brothers again. You're not a member of this club, but you belong to us. You *belong* to me. Don't forget your place again." He turns back to Cheryl. "Bring Matt here for lunch tomorrow. He needs to be informed of *his* place, and I don't trust that you're capable of doing that informing on your own anymore."

"Well that makes two of us with trust issues." I remove my arms from his neck. "I know you're hurting right now, but stop taking it out on me. And stop focusing so much on where I'm at and who I'm with because it's making you miss what's happening all around you. It's allowing people like *Warren* to walk in your front door. There was a time he wouldn't have driven down this street. So until you're ready to tell me what secrets you're keeping about him, I'll be with Matt."

Gary and I haven't really ever fought before. We have tiffs, like everyone does, but there's a weight pressing down on us, a smothering pressure that's cutting off our ability to communicate. He's holding out on me, I can feel the omissions. Yet none of the Leidolf will talk to me about anything related to Gary or to the murders.

Their ostracizing silence makes me not want to be at the bar, and it feels weird not to wake up there again, but waking up next to Matt, the two of us stone-cold sober in his tiny bed, I'm able to shrug off all my troublesome emotions and focus on a single thread of happiness.

I sit up, one knee folded over Matt's and the other leg pressed against the wall. "Gary invited you to have lunch with us today."

He tucks a hand behind his head and lifts a brow. "Are you officially introducing me to your family?"

I shrug. "More like Gary wants to approve who I'm spending my time with because Samantha's murder has his head all shook up."

He sighs. "So he normally doesn't have to approve of your boyfriends, I'm just getting special scrutiny because of the murders?"

I smile. "I wouldn't know. I haven't had a *boyfriend* since I was eighteen."

He rolls onto his side. "That was about four years ago, right?"

I shrug. "Thereabout. But it was a long-term thing. I basically spent my whole life with the same person, planning and dreaming of a future that the guy just up and walked away from. Gary knew him, and when the boy left me behind like nothing about me mattered to him—not my dreams, not our plans that I'd worked two jobs to afford, and most definitely not the love I had for him—Gary was there for that. So maybe he does want to scare you a little so you don't break my heart."

He cups my thigh. "Who's going to keep you from breaking mine?"

No matter which way I spin Matt inside my brain, he's the exception to every truth I thought I knew about men. I touch his face, the planes of his jaw firm under my palm. This man is art, and he's mine. "I think you're right. We need a place of our own."

He smiles. "Is this your way of making up for bailing on me all day yesterday?"

I shrug, feeling guilty for having told him I'd come straight back. After my tiff with Gary, I'd showered and met Chopper in the hallway between his and Gary's apartments. He informed me there was something needing attention in my office. I trotted down the stairs and entered my office to find a quarter of a million dollars waiting for me. So I had no choice but to bail on Matt. I had to spend the day accounting for the money, recording it in my pen and paper ledger, and writing up a deposit schedule for amounts that could be added to what the bar brings in each day. After breaking the money into stacks, marking each of them appropriately and situating them in the safe, it was well after dark before I knocked on Matt's back door. I couldn't help but feel warm when noting that the concrete pad had been swept clear of debris. "Is moving in with you a good apology?"

"The best." He grins. "Can we go out looking for rentals today?"

I hug my knees to my chest. "I bought my house with the intention of fixing it up to sell, but I haven't done enough to make a profit on it yet so I have the loan payment there each month. Then, if I sell the house, Beth won't have a place to live."

"Is she part owner?" he asks. I shake my head and he sighs. "Does she pay rent?"

I rest my chin on my knees. "No. That's one reason I haven't bothered to fix the place up much. Until she gets her feet under her, I can't sell."

He pulls himself forward and tucks his chin against the front of my legs, eyes looking up into mine. "We've got problems then because I hate us being cramped in this bed, and I know you do too. So what's our solution?" His fingers glide along the curve of my calf. "I want a full kitchen to cook for you in, and a tub to bathe you in, and a nice big bed to love you in."

I smile. "Is that what we're doing? Love?"

He topples us over, fitting his body against mine. "I fell in love with you somewhere between hello and waking up next to you that first morning. So love is *absolutely* what I'm doing."

"I think it's what I'm doing, too."

His brow lifts. "You think?"

I grin. "Your body is a little too distracting for me to be sure. Could just be a severe case of lust."

"I'll give you lust." He buries his face in my neck, beginning a familiar path of devouring down my body. My phone rings. *It's your sister calling. Answer. Answer. Answer!* bleats out twice before Matt gets up with a frustrated huff and yanks my phone from the charging port beside the bed.

"Sorry." I smile as he drops the phone on my stomach and resumes his position, his mouth making up for lost time. "Beth, I'm busy, and I really hate the stupid ringtone you put on my phone." I bite down, gritting my teeth as Matt runs his mouth over every spot I have. "I've got to go."

"Wait!" she yells. "Cheryl is dead!"

"What?" I sit up, pulling the sheets over me to get Matt to stop. "How? When?"

"Mom just called," Beth cries. "They found her… she's… gutted."

My phone slips from my fingers, Beth's voice shaking the air around me but not penetrating my skull. Matt's hand cups my shoulder, his other picking up the phone to get the information from Beth himself. I can't move. Cheryl is only seventeen.

Matt tugs on his clothes and pulls the dress I wore yesterday over my head. "Beth said everyone's meeting at your parents' house. You're supposed to get Gary. Can you do that?" He dips down to look into my eyes.

I shake my head. "I just saw her yesterday. She was practicing her song for Samantha's funeral."

He frowns. "At the bar?"

"While breakfast was still being served." I recall the smell of bacon. I don't know about the first four murders, but these last two, these are *Gary's* family. "I'm not safe. No one is."

~20~

Cheryl was a songbird, one set to pay tribute to a woman who spent her whole life battling demons. Even before Samantha turned to drugs, she dealt with an abusive alcoholic father. Same as Cheryl. I make the connection for Matt, telling him what I know of both women's lives while he drives us to my parents' house. He suggests I let Chief know my theory because a killer targeting girls raised by abusive fathers is as good of a straw to grasp as any.

Chief answers my call, but not to listen to what I have to say. He tells me there is more than one witness putting Cheryl on the back of Gary's bike yesterday morning, and one of her meth-head neighbors said they saw him drop her off and that he'd gone inside the small brick house she'd managed to keep paying rent on after her dad went to jail for his third DUI. The house is on a dead-end street just past two rundown trailers and a caved-in doublewide. I imagine Gary did go inside. He'd want to check the place since it's a bad neighborhood and Cheryl has been living there alone. Her deadbeat boyfriend moved in the day her dad went to jail, but the kid recently picked up and left town, taking anything of Cheryl's that had any value at all.

I explain all this to Chief. Even tell him about the conflict between Gary and Cheryl's dad, a conflict that has more to do with my own dad than anything else. Cheryl was born to a man just as weak as the one I was born to, the difference being mine wields some kind of power over hers, so by default, Cheryl was never allowed to come into the bar. She'd sneak, of course, and we'd all make a fuss over her because you didn't just see the star shining brightly in her, you felt it. But because Gary was the last person seen with her, Chief stopped him and Chopper when they were away from the bar this morning. That's why I couldn't find them earlier, and it's why they never returned my messages. Gary has been arrested for Cheryl's murder, and Chief intends to hold Chopper for as long as he can.

"We need a pie chart up here," Dad announces shortly after Matt and I take a seat in his living room. He's in front of the dingy bay window, standing tall and proud like he's the leader of some great pack when in reality, he's five foot eight and only empowered by the ample supply of children and weak-minded adults who want to be led by the loudest mouth in the room.

I roll my eyes, unsure of how I even got here. A part of me knew Matt was driving to my parents' place, but that part was too numb to stop him. Now I'm sitting here looking into my dad's face. "What are you going to chart? Your favorite pie flavors?"

His eyes narrow, leveling on me. He doesn't like to be challenged, especially by a female. Especially by *me*. But Matt is beside me and Dad doesn't know how this new man I brought into the fold will react to any badmouthing, so he breaks eye contact and looks at the people he *can* influence. "I'm going to chart all the men in this town and find out which one killed our Cheryl."

I slip my hand into Matt's and pull him to his feet with me. "I'm going to go ahead and put my money on the law figuring out the riddle before you and your chart of pies does."

Dad's face reddens. "Too good to help your own family? Go run off like you always do and act like you're better than us when your blood is the same as ours. The same as *Cheryl's*."

I approach him. "The only person I act like I'm better than is *you*, because *everyone* is better than you. I also support my family. If you'd like to debate that fact, I'll go call those bikers who haven't hung you from the John Henry statue simply because *I* keep them from doing so, and let them weigh in on exactly *who* my family is and *how* I treat them."

Matt's hand snakes around my waist. He's letting me fight my own battles while showing his support, a sentiment Dad knows nothing about. He turns away from Matt's wall of supportive muscle, muttering as if he's unaffected by my and Matt's dominance. "The cops don't care about anyone in this town, so to get justice for our Cheryl, we'll have to take matters into our own hands."

"Yeah, because *you* care about this town." I can't help myself, I have to call out his bullcrap. "And when's the last time *you* talked to *our* Cheryl?"

Fire rages in his eyes, but he clamps his mouth shut. He doesn't know what kind of man Matt is but he knows what kind of woman I am. If he pushes me, I'll make his teeth bleed. And he doesn't want that kind of confrontation in front of everyone. He only does confrontation when he knows he can win. "You don't care about anyone but yourself, *Dad*. And I'm not going to let you use Cheryl's murder as a platform to push your own agenda. However you're planning to make yourself look good, and whoever you're planning to stomp on while you do it, it better steer clear of me and mine because if Gary gets served up on your plate of pie, I'll come for you, and I won't be alone."

"Enough!" Mom steps between us, eyes pleading. "He's only trying to help, Tessa. That's all any of us are doing!"

Beth moves to Mom's right shoulder. "I saw Cheryl about a week ago, just before I heard about Samantha. How about we go around the room and all say when we saw her last? And Dad can chart that on his…graph."

I train my eyes on Mom. "Or, we could just go around the room and say the names of any men we think are capable of murder. Like the one who left me with fond memories of gunshots ringing out when his wife hid from him so he'd stop beating her. Only a sadistic man would fire guns beside her children's heads and hold knives to their throats, all to torture his wife further."

Mom gasps and Dad pales, neither of them used to anyone talking about his dirty deeds out loud. The voices around us begin to raise and Beth puts up her hands. "Who says it's a man? The killer could be a woman."

Matt shifts, arm moving up to wrap around my shoulders. "Statistically, women aren't violent murderers. If they kill, they usually poison."

Voices behind us change to arguing about whether or not Matt is right. Mom and Beth join in, the fifteen people in this room suddenly becoming detectives with the nose of an FBI profiler. I pierce Dad with a cold stare. "Thanks for the information, Matt. Maybe poison is what I'll use the next time a man takes a sledgehammer to the windows of his wife's car when she finally gets brave enough to load her babies up and leave him."

"Mark my words," Dad sneers. "It'll end up being one of Gary's thugs that's killing our women."

"No one who's been murdered has been *yours*, and the only reason you're against Gary is because he and his aren't afraid of *you*."

I storm out of the house and through the muddy yard, not willing to stay in this place any longer. Matt tugs me to a stop. "Your dad…all that stuff you said—"

"All true, and no, I don't want to talk about it." I pull his car door open. "I need to get back to the bar. I should never have left."

"Come here." He stops me from getting into the seat, pulling me into a hug and pressing his face into my neck. "If I would have known, I wouldn't have brought you here. Beth said… I didn't know about your dad."

I close my eyes and lean into his hug. "No one really knows the extent of what he is. Not even Gary, so keep it to yourself."

He pulls away from my neck and stares at my face. "I'll promise to keep it to myself if you promise me that when we're not together, you'll keep in touch and stay in public places." He rests his forehead on mine. "We'll stay together at night, my place or yours, until we figure out what to do about getting a place of our own. Through the day, you'll stay where gobs of people can see you. All the time. Promise me."

I nod to where Randy is parked at the end of the driveway. "I have shadows all around me, and the more I'm away from the bar, the thinner it spreads them. Let's get back. I need to figure out how we're going to get Gary and Chopper out of jail."

~21~

I didn't have to tell the club that Gary and Chopper had been picked up. They knew already. Gary's one phone call was placed to the bar, and Chief let him make the call as soon as they arrived at the police station. Part of his reasoning would have been to keep the Leidolf calm, but it doesn't make any sense that he picked Gary up so quickly after discovering Cheryl's body.

"What are you not telling me, Chief?" I call him as I motion Matt around to the back of the Grille, rolling down the window to wave at Brian so he'll let Matt pass.

"Tessa," Chief grumbles. "I *can't* discuss this investigation with you. And even if I could, Gary's darn near forbade it."

"Gary told you not to talk to me?"

He sighs. "Gary's worried about you. Like the rest of us are."

"Yet you're arresting my cousin? And…colluding?"

I hear the squeak of his chair in the background, his voice coming out lower. "Tessa, I don't have a *choice* in this arrest. People are talking. Naming names. And the only thing keeping Gary out of jail for Samantha's murder was Warren's alibi. But your boyfriend pulled the plug on that this morning, called ten minutes after Cheryl was found and said he lied. And it wasn't *me* he called. So go figure out who *Warren* is colluding with." He hangs up on me.

I stare at my phone while Matt parks as close to the rhododendron that borders his building as he can. "Warren's the guy you slapped, right?"

91

I take a breath, wondering if I should have let that call be on speaker. "Now you see why I slapped him."

He shrugs. "Why would he frame Gary? To cover his own tracks?"

I get out of the car and take Matt's hand, bringing him in the bar with me. "Warren's an idiot, but he's not a murderer, so I don't know why he's lying."

Matt's hand tightens on mine as we enter the hallway. "You sure you're not letting your past with him skew your opinions? He's your ex-boyfriend, right?"

I stop and stare at him. "My feelings for Warren have been dead for years. Except for the hatred. So I'm not denying his ability to be a murderer to protect him."

"Your feelings can't be that dead." He huffs. "Beth said you two have some *cosmic* draw."

I remove my hand from his. "Is that why it's been so easy to stay away from Warren for the last four years?"

He chews the inside of his cheek, trying to hide his grin. "I guess he's not much of a destiny if I'm the one you're kind of in love with now."

I pat his jaw. "Exactly. And when did Beth tell you this fable of hers?"

He shrugs. "She didn't so much tell me as I overheard her saying it to someone the night of that meeting. It was another reason I went out to find a bottle of vodka and got persuaded to follow you when I saw your car. I felt like I'd been broken up with before I ever had a chance to take you on a date."

The back door opens and I cringe. Montrose fills the doorway. He's the head of a northern charter and the few times we've met, we've not gotten along. And with Gary and Chopper in jail, he'll take senior spot with the other members. As much as I support the Leidolf as a whole, I only vouch for *our* charter members. Some of the others aren't as straightforward, and they're not nearly as laid back. I move Matt along the hall and push him into my office. "I need you to stay here for a few minutes because things are about to get real messy and I'd like both of us to live long enough to go on a lot more dates…or one, since I'm not sure what we've done so far can be considered a date."

I press a kiss to Matt's lips and dart back into the hallway where Montrose and ten of his men are talking with Brian, Zeno and Randy. I turn toward the bar and run smack into Chopper. "Oh my gosh!" I throw my arms around his neck. He holds me tight, fingers digging into my back while he lifts me off my feet and slides us into my office.

Matt clears his throat. Chopper's grip loosens but he doesn't let go. "What's he doing back here?"

I pull from Chopper's arms, cupping his face as tears stream down mine. "I was with him when Beth called to tell me about Cheryl. Then I called Chief and he said… I've been so worried. Are you okay? Is Gary here?"

"No." Chopper pulls me forward, his lips on my ear. "I've got to go to the sanctuary. Get rid of this kid, and then wait for me upstairs." He moves his face to mine. "Now. My apartment. Nowhere else."

I nod and wipe my eyes. He presses a kiss to my forehead and closes the door behind him. "That was intimate," Matt grumbles.

I turn to him, taking his hands in mine and meeting his gaze. "Next to Gary and Beth, Chopper is someone I'm very close to. We have a type of love for one another that's probably hard for most people to understand, but how I feel about him is *not* how I feel about you. I've just known him for a whole lot longer." I stare at our hands, heart pounding because I felt the way Chopper's was beating under his shirt. He's spooked, and that terrifies me. "I've got to do something for club, Matt. Will you wait for me next door?"

His shoulders slump. "You're kicking me out?"

Tears weigh heavy on my lashes. "I don't have a choice. Chopper said you have to go and…something is happening. I don't know what, exactly, but it's something not giving me any time to say goodbye to you. You have to leave. Now. Go out the front door."

"My car is parked in the back."

I fish his keys out of his pocket. "I'll have someone pull it around front."

He wipes my tears, voice softening. "Come with me, Tessa. You don't need to stay here in the middle of whatever this is. You don't belong here."

I look away and then let go of him, opening my door and checking to make sure all the men from the hallway have entered the sanctuary. They have, and the door is closed. Church is in session. I reach back a hand and Matt slips his palm into mine. I tug him along the corridor and out into the main bar. "I'll call you as soon as I can." I press my lips to his and turn away, slipping back into the corridor before he has a chance to say anything. Not every member of the Leidolf is in the sanctuary, so there's no way Matt will be allowed to re-enter this part of the building.

Moving quickly, the urgency I felt in Chopper's chest driving my haste, I traverse the hallway and reach the stairs. "Tessa." My name rolls off a thick tongue. I didn't see Bear come in with Montrose but there's no mistaking that drawl. He thinks women like it and that if he sticks his meaty tongue in my ear *I'll* like it. That way of thinking got more than his ego bruised the last time he was here.

I contemplate ignoring him, moving on up the stairs and locking myself in Chopper's apartment, but the one thing I know not to show is fear. I face him and force a smile. "How was the ride down?"

"You look like you've been cryin', sugar. I can help you dry those tears."

I steel my nerves. "My cousin getting out of jail will dry them."

His lips tip up. "Montrose wants to talk to you about that." He steps aside and sweeps his hand back down the hall I just came from. "After you."

~22~

I've never been in the sanctuary before. As far as I know, it's forbidden to have a non-club member inside. Chopper doesn't say anything when Bear pushes me through the door but I see the lines around his eyes deepen. He's not happy I'm here.

Montrose is at one end of an oversized oblong table. There are chairs and benches around the room and even a podium, not unlike what you'd see in an actual church. But what's in view isn't the entirety of this room. The wall to my left was added after Gary bought the place. He reinforced the entire room with steel panels but he brought that wall in about five feet. I know this because my office is on the other side of that wall and behind a seemingly heavy old-school filing cabinet, there's a door. The lock on it leads to the first safe. The place we keep the money. Behind that safe is the larger door of the second safe. I don't know the code for it but I did see it before it was in use. I suspect that's where Gary keeps the guns. Both the ones they traffic, and the ones the club uses when they need them.

I don't presume to approach the table. I pick a spot on the wall where I'll be able to watch Chopper's face, and I stand perfectly still. There are now eighteen men in the room, nine from Gary's charter and nine from Montrose's, and they're all staring at me. "I hear you're in tight with the chief of police." Montrose's gravely voice scratches along my spine.

"I'm tight with the Leidolf," I answer. Chopper's head moves almost imperceptibly. He doesn't want me taking a *tone* with Montrose, I'm to be *nice*. I take a breath. "Chief and I were friends until he arrested Gary. Now he isn't talking to me much, but he's said enough for me to know the cops are going to try to pin all the murders on one person."

Montrose's head tilts. "That's why I'm here. We're going to give them that person."

My back straightens. "Not Gary."

Disgust seeps from his pores. "Little girl, Gary is my brother before he's anything to you. The men here aren't friends of the wolf, we *are* the wolves. *You* are prey."

A noise rumbles from Chopper's chest. Montrose glances at him. The sound is clear, anyone wanting to mess with me will have to go through Chopper. Not that I wasn't already under his protection, or any of the other members of Gary's charter, but Chopper is making a distinction. I am his. Which is going to make explaining my relationship with Matt real fun.

Montrose pushes his chair back, agitation ticking his jaw. "We've been dealing the police hands for longer than you've been alive, *Tessa*, so tell us exactly what your police friend has told you, then you can go fetch us some drinks."

I bite back the urge to tell him where I'll shove those drinks. "Chief Dunbar implied that he's being pressured to make an arrest and had no choice but to pick up Gary after several witnesses placed Cheryl on Gary's bike, and another said he saw Gary go inside Cheryl's house." I don't tell them about Warren. Only what I think they probably already know because something is off about Chopper's demeanor. He wants me out of this room. "If you have specific questions, I'll try to get Chief to answer them, but he's only answered two of my calls today and hung up on me both times."

Bear flattens a palm over his heart. "Our family is your family. We're gonna to take care of this for you, sugar."

Randy nods, looking around the table at Montrose's men. "We appreciate the extra manpower. When Samantha was killed, we weren't sure if it was because of her connection to Gary. To us. But now we have another. Whether the killer means it to be or not, Cheryl's attack is personal, and it's against *all* Leidolf."

A prick of rot festers through my gut. Either these two attacks aren't related to the other four, or Gary was connected to the other victims. His shirt being found with Layla's body beats against my skull. I press my hands into the wall and steady myself. I can't say any of this out loud. My cousin is *not* a murderer.

Chopper leaves his seat and presses himself around me, hand tightening on my hips until it hurts. His eyes are cold and hard. "Send Zeno with the beer, then wait for me in my room." I nod, tears filling my eyes at the roughness of his touch. I want to hit him, scream at him, but if he's hurting me, he has a reason. "Go," he growls, letting me out of his grip. I rush from the room and break for the stairs. I'll text Zeno from upstairs. But not one second before I'm barricaded inside Chopper's apartment.

~

Pacing Chopper's floor, I watch the clock. Fifty minutes have passed since I locked myself inside this room like a scared little kid. I don't even know why I'm afraid, other than the fact that Chopper is acting weird. I pull the waist of my jeans out and check my hip. As I suspected, there's bruising.

I take Matt's keys out of my pocket and shoot him a text. *Be in front of your building in four minutes. Not five minutes. Four.* Unbolting Chopper's door, I crack it open and listen. It's quiet. Stepping into the hall, I tread softly until I make it to the stairs. I stop again and listen. Voices can be heard, but none of them sound close. All I need is a clear shot down the stairs and out the back door. Then I have to get by whoever is guarding the parking lot.

Taking a deep breath, I spring down the steps and rush out the door, running to Matt's car and ducking into the driver's seat without bothering to glance up. I throw the car into gear and back out of the space. Swiveling my head in the other direction, I don't see anyone. I bring the front of the car around and hit the gas. I don't know what's happening with the club today, but I'm technically not ditching them since they're not out here watching the lot.

I head down the alley and make the turn. Matt is locking the door to his office. I pull to the curb and blow the horn, watching the rearview for a tail. Matt's eyes narrow as he opens the passenger door. "What's going on, Tessa?"

"Get in!" I yell.

He drops into the passenger seat and grapples for the dash as I take off, squealing his tires a little as I head for the nearest side street. "Geez, Tessa! What's going on? Where are we going?"

"We're going to hunt down a liar whose destiny is to have the sole of my boot permanently affixed to his face."

~23~

Matt's quiet as I steer us toward the edge of town, out to where Warren somehow managed to buy enough land to set up a full bells-n-whistles mechanic's shop. I drove by the place right after I heard the shop was opening. As far as I know, Warren took some automotive classes at a vocational school during his high school years but never did anything with that knowledge. And he sure as heck doesn't have the capital to open up a modern garage like the one gleaming in the sun up ahead of me. Even the oval sign with orange lettering saying *Town's End Auto* is too nice for Warren's cheap pockets. He's in bed with someone, and it isn't his current girlfriend.

Since I was last by here, the parking lot has been paved and a little building with vending machines is labeled *Snack Shack.* Four garage bay doors are attached to a long two-story building that connects them with one oversized garage bay. Three of the four doors on the one side are open, and the one labeled *Quick Oil* has a car lifted over a pit. Warren's cousin Jimmy is underneath that car while Warren leans over the side of a Pontiac two bays away. I send Chopper a text. ***I'm with Matt. Will be back soon.***

That text won't smooth anything over with him, but he manhandled me today so I figure we're even. I slip the phone into my pocket and lean across the console, placing a kiss on Matt's scowling lips. "I'm sorry about earlier, and for driving

100

your car like I stole it. I wanted to make sure no one followed us."

"You should have left with me this afternoon instead of kicking me out."

"You're probably right." I sigh. "Wait here. I need to handle something."

He swallows. "Can I at least get out and stretch my legs? Or am I just supposed to sit here like your lap dog?"

I move back to my side of the car and open the door. "If you want to fight, Matt, I'm all for it. Just wait until I rip out this snake's tongue and strangle him with it, then I'm all yours."

I slam Matt's door and march in Warren's direction. He glances up, head doing a double-take before it starts shaking. "Whatever you're selling, I already have plenty of it, Tessa. So go back to wherever you came from and stay out of my sight the way I'm staying out of yours."

He keeps working, eyes on whatever he's tinkering with under the hood. I enter the bay and take hold of the hood. He jumps back, eyes wide as the hood slams closed. "Are you out of your mind?"

"You know as well as I do that Gary didn't kill anyone," I shout.

"Of course I know that!" He plunks his wrench into a toolbox. "Why do you think I lied for him to start with?"

"I don't know, Warren. Why did you?"

He rubs his face, smearing grease through his five o'clock shadow. "I was trying to help him out."

"You've never done a single thing in your life out of the kindness of your heart so the lie you just told me is the second one I know of you telling *today*," I snarl. "I have no doubt there are plenty more, but all I care about is justice for Gary. I want the truth, Warren. Why are you so involved in this case that you get to be the one saying whether or not Gary goes to jail?"

He moves toward me. "Chief is the one arresting an innocent man, so why don't you take your pretty little self on down to his office. He always was glad to see you coming. And going."

"If you're looking to be slapped again, I'll do it without provocation. All your greasy little self has to do is ask."

"I've had enough of your hands being on me." He shoos me away. "Get on out of here. I've got work to do."

I stay where I am. "Trust me, I don't want to be here any more than you want me here, but you're the one who lied. *I* could have given Gary an alibi for Samantha and stuck to it, but now I'm the one looking like a liar because you just up and decided to stick your nose where it didn't belong. Again."

"I already told you, I was trying to help him."

"Why? What's Gary to you that you think you're all the help he has?"

His arms fold. "I know I'm not all he has but despite *you*, Gary's always been fair to me."

"And you repay him by screwing up the only chance he has of putting up a real alibi?"

"I didn't think it would go this far!" He throws his hands through his hair and turns, catching sight of Matt, who is leaning on the side of his car watching us. Warren's jaw works as he brings his stare back to mine. "You haven't changed a bit, Tessa. Still stubborn as a mule and not willing to hear anything anyone has to say."

"My hearing is just fine. It's the talking that's the problem. I'll have to ask Marcie if she has that problem with you, too. I *hear* she just dumped you, so I'm sure she'll give an honest opinion."

His chestnut-brown eyes narrow. "Better to ask Marcie than that skank of a sister you've got."

I step toward him, nostrils flaring. "Talk about my sister one more time."

His lip curls. "Too bad Beth doesn't defend *you* like this. When it's your name in the mud, it's usually her doing the slinging."

My insides freeze. I used to confide in him when I'd hear something Beth had said about me behind my back. He knows all the parts of me that hurt, so my excuse is weak, but I mutter it anyway. "You don't know her like I do."

He backs away. "I know her plenty."

My teeth clench. "Trust me, I heard *plenty* about all the ways you got to know her. In *my* van."

He stares at me, tension building a bomb between us. But *this* isn't the fuse I'm here to ignite. "Stay out of Gary's business or I'll slit your throat myself." I march past him, purposefully bumping him as I pass.

Matt's eyebrow cocks as I near. "Didn't go well?"

"Drive." I go to the passenger door and plop into the seat, catching sight of Warren's body leaned back over the Pontiac. It didn't take him long to get that hood back open and I shouldn't be surprised. Every time I've depended on him, he's let me down, so I don't know why I expected to get the truth out of him this time. He's not capable of doing the right thing.

Matt starts his engine and stares at me. "Where to?"

I check my phone. Chopper's words make the hair on my neck raise. *Your house. Now.* I slip a sweaty hand onto Matt's knee. "Let's go to my place."

$$\sim24\sim$$

I'm glad things didn't work out between Warren and me, he's no Matt Honaker. And now that I'm experiencing Matt, I can't believe I ever fell for Warren. But with the way Warren's name has been coming up and the fact that I've occupied the same space as him, I can't help remembering the scratch of his voice against my ear and the feel of his skin on mine. Memories I've drunk to forget, and ones I've tried to use other men to forget.

"You okay?" Matt's hand slips across the console as we drive down my street.

I nod. "It's just been a long day."

His fingers tighten on mine. "That is has. And we have some things to talk about. But I don't want to fight with you, so let's take the night to sleep on everything and then we'll have a conversation tomorrow about how you're not going to keep bossing me around." He tilts his eyes to mine, a grin tugging at his lips. "When we get to your house, I'll make us some food, and then I'll take my boss to bed. Sound like a plan?"

My throat tightens. I have no idea if Chopper is waiting for me. Of all the times to start a relationship, this is the worst. But I'm in deep with Matt, moving at lightning speed and no part of me wants to slow down. I manage a smile for him. "Your plan sounds perfect."

His palm opens as Brian's bike comes into view. Matt tries to pull away but I hold him tight until his fingers close back over mine. "You knew I came with shadows, so don't get mad that they're around. Especially now, when a murderer is running loose."

Matt turns into the driveway and parks behind Beth's car. "I get that tensions are running high, Tessa. Especially for those guys." He nods toward Brian. "Gary's arrest is a big deal for all of you, but I'm in this, too. I'm *with* you. And I'm *scared* for you." He places a hand along my jaw. "I know you don't want to hear anything bad said about the club, but after today, I can't help but tell you that I don't like the way they treat you. It's like you're property to them. They tell you what to do, where to go, *who* you can go there with." He swallows. "I want what's best for you, babe, and I'm not sure that's them."

"Maybe I'm not what's good for you then." I place my hand over his. "You're mad that I'm bossing you around, and that's basically what you're saying the club does to me."

He grimaces as another bike shows up. It's Zeno, and I don't have to look to know. "We're not in normal times, Matt. The Leidolf aren't usually like this, but I probably am."

He smiles and slips his big hand around the back of my neck, pulling me to his lips. "Things are slow at the office right now so I'm happy to ride your shotgun anytime, or drive you anywhere you need to go, because I'd rather you be with me than any of them." His mouth closes over mine, sensual and sweet. "I'm all the protection you need, Tessa. Now let's get you inside so you can eat, and then we can *both* release some tension."

~Matt~

Tessa left at dawn, on the back of Chopper's bike after his text woke her up. I spent some time with Beth and then left for my office, hoping to meet up with Tessa for lunch. She hasn't answered any of my texts, though.

I call her on my short walk to the Grille, leaving a message as I enter the building. I walk to where there's a gate in the bar and crane my neck to see down the hall to where her office is. One of the tall blonde twins who bartend here steps in front of my view. "What can I get for you?"

I shove my phone in my pocket. "I'm looking for Tessa. Is she in her office?"

"Not at the moment." She shrugs. "I'll tell her you stopped by."

"How about I just wait right here for my *girlfriend*." I let her know that I have a right to be looking down that hallway, and sit on the nearest stool so I can do just that, because Tessa may very well be back there and this twin just isn't saying.

A snicker reaches my ear and I turn right, watching four members of the Leidolf mock me. I turn back to the blonde. "I'll take a beer while I wait for Tessa. Anything you have on tap will do."

She saunters off to get my drink and I glance to the men. They're smiling at me, laughter on the edge of their lips. A ball of annoyance forms in my chest. Seeing how I don't know where my supposed girlfriend even is, there's not much I can say to shut them up.

I take out my phone and shoot Tessa another message. A shadow of another person catches the corner of my eye. It's Warren. He has a ballcap pulled low over his face but everything about Tessa's ex is burned into my memory. It's him. In her bar. Talking to her wolves.

"Liar!" Her screech hits my ears. I swing around, expecting Tessa to be charging this direction but I don't see her. I get off the stool. The blonde blocks my path again, her eyes flicking to the men at the end of the bar. I turn to them and the older one nods. The blonde moves aside and lets me pass.

I enter the hall and catch a wisp of Tessa's hair pushing through her office door. Chopper is standing in the doorway of what they call a sanctuary. Our eyes lock, words passing unsaid. He nods toward her door and then slips behind his, shutting it. I turn to the wood slab beside me and knock. "Tessa? Babe, it's me. Open up."

She throws the door open, eyes red. "Matt." She pulls me inside and slams the door, fingers twisting the lock before she plows past me, dropping into the chair at her desk.

I sink to my knees beside her, smoothing a hand over her thigh. "Babe, what's going on? Why are you crying? And who lied to you?"

She doesn't answer, pressing her finger onto the sensor of her keyboard to unlock her computer. She clicks through a menu. I spin her chair, forcing her to look at me. "What's going on?"

She wipes her face. "They're liars. All of them."

"The Leidolf?" I question. "It doesn't surprise me, but what exactly did they lie to you about?"

She crosses her arms, teeth grinding. "They have contacts in the regional jail. Ever since Gary was transferred there, the guys have been in communication with him because he was given access to a cell phone." Her nostrils flare as she pulls air through her fiery chest. "Supposedly he called and said we're to work with Warren. Let him inside this building, and work with him."

"Work with him on what?"

Tears storm her eyes. "On clearing Gary's name. *My* cousin's name. But Gary wouldn't do this to me. I *know* he wouldn't allow Warren to be here."

I scrub a hand over my jaw. "Are they saying Gary thinks Warren knows who's killing people? Because then it would make sense for Gary to order the club to let Warren in."

Her head shakes, eyes lowering to stare at her hands. "I don't know what they think Warren knows, but I do know Gary wouldn't allow him in this bar. That's why…" Her eyes shift to the locked door. "I'm going to clear Gary's name myself."

I stand and bring her to her feet, adjusting myself into the chair and settling her on my lap. "Babe, I know you want to help Gary. And I know him being locked up is painful for you. But there's not much you can do for him. If he's innocent, the police will figure that out and let him go."

"If?" she bites.

I rest a hand along her cheek. "I'm not the enemy. I'm only trying to help you."

Her body whirls around, fingers flying over her keyboard. A camera feed of her office pops onto the screen. I lean over her shoulder and find the angle, looking up to a stack of books atop a shelf in the corner. The camera is somewhere up there. "I thought the bar didn't have cameras inside."

"This is the only interior camera." Her hard eyes meet mine. "No one knows I installed this. I keep sensitive files in here so I wanted a camera, just in case anything ever happened." She turns back to the laptop and scrolls through the motion sensor footage.

"What exactly are you looking for?"

"Gary." She huffs. "I need something with a time stamp to prove where he was when Samantha and Cheryl were murdered. If I can find footage of him in here…" Her jaw sets. "All I need is footage. I'll doctor the time stamp or say my camera time is wrong."

I steady my hands and cup her shoulders. "Babe, I assume the reason no one knows about this camera is because the Leidolf will go through the roof if they find out. So before you go and get yourself in hot water with the club *and* with the law, walk out into the Grille with me and find out why Gary *might* have actually asked his men to work with the weasel." I brace for her reaction. "Warren is in the bar."

~25~

It was all I could do to keep up with Tessa as she weaved and dodged through the crowd on the warpath to confront Warren. Gripping her shoulders, I stand behind her, holding her from him while staring the man down. He isn't looking at me. His eyes are on her. "I'm here because Gary asked me to be."

"Liar!" she screams, the pain of betrayal shaking her voice.

Warren's eyes move to where my fingers are curled around her shoulders. I lower my mouth to her ear, whispering calming words. His gaze lifts to where my lips fit against her lobe. He most certainly still has feelings for her. I place a kiss on the soft flesh of her neck and straighten, my point made. She's with me.

He shifts uncomfortably in his seat. "I just came from the jail, Tessa. Gary told me with his own mouth to get down here."

"It's true," confirms one of the men who had a good laugh at my expense earlier. He's chewing on the end of what used to be a cigarette.

She turns on him. "There's no way this lying rat was allowed to see Gary when *I* can't even get in to see him!"

I clear my throat. "I'll take you to the jail tomorrow, babe. If anyone has been allowed in to see Gary, they'll have a record of it. And maybe you'll get to see him, too."

Warren's arms cross. "There's no record of me being there. Someone owed me a favor, and I called it in."

She breaks free of my grip, lunging for his throat. Chopper steps in front of her, shoving her back into my arms. My eyes

109

narrow. Chopper stares at me, seemingly expressionless, but there's no mistaking his challenge. Or the menace in the words coming from my left. They slice through the tension. "If another murder happens while Gary's in jail, they'll let him go. I think we can arrange taking care of a problem female."

Chopper turns to the man. Other members do as well. He laughs. "I wasn't talking about Gary's little cousin. But I imagine we can find *someone* to break our rules for."

Tessa tugs from my hands and rounds on him. "Whose going to do this killing, Montrose? You?" Her teeth show through her grin. "Because I'd love to see you try."

He gets off his stool and faces Warren, who is now out of his seat and flanking Chopper. "Maybe *he* should do it. Earn his keep."

"His keep?" Tessa balks. "Warren isn't joining the Leidolf!"

Warren steps in front of her. "You're not the boss of what or *who* I do, sweetheart."

She lunges and I get an arm around her waist, pulling her kicking body tightly against me. She gives up on escaping and leans as far toward Warren as she can. "Why is it that only women have to die? I nominate *you* as Montrose's victim."

He smiles. "If you're going to be the one pulling the trigger, I accept. You never could hit the broad side of a barn."

"That's enough," Chopper roars. "Gary's word is to let him be, so let him be, Tessa."

The men all watch her. Her back goes rigid but she remains still in my arms, her eyes locked in battle with Warren's. "I'm going to find out what got you a place in this bar and when I do, I'm going to turn you into ash. You hear me, Warren? I'm going to burn down your world."

He looks away and I slide onto the seat of the booth behind me, holding Tessa tightly against my side. Chopper stands in front of her, blocking her way out. "Warren has information. You need to hear it."

He gives Warren a signal and I look around the Grille. It's devoid of people. I've noticed the bar being closed at unexpected times, and they must have closed while I was in Tessa's office. I glance at Warren. He's standing to Chopper's left, angled toward the rest of the men while Chopper stares at Tessa. "They found a bat outside Cheryl's house. About a hundred feet into the woods. There's a partial bloody fingerprint on it that matches to Gary. And another on a piece of glove that was found. A glove like the ones used in the kitchen here."

I feel wetness on my arm and lean around to look at Tessa's face. She's crying again. I hold her tighter.

Her head shakes and she looks up at Warren. He meets her eyes and nods. "I saw the bat. It's yours."

"Hers?" I question.

Her body trembles. "I made that bat in high school. Gary used to carry it around, strapped to his bike. Now he keeps it in his room." Her eyes float to mine. "My name is carved into it, so if Warren saw it…"

Even without her name carved into it, Warren would know that bat was hers because they were together in high school. He's probably the reason she took a shop class to begin with. I shift uncomfortably. "Who are you, Warren? What gives you special access to Gary and to all the evidence?"

His nostrils flare. "I've been in this town a heck of a lot longer than you, *that's* who I am."

Tessa scoffs. "Chief hates Warren just as much as the rest of us, but Warren's a rat, sneaking in and out of everywhere without a single loyalty to anyone around him. Hard to tell what he did to get today's privileges, but eventually, all rats are smashed." She glares at him. "Any more news to share, rat? Or have you overstayed your welcome so soon?"

Chopper doesn't allow an answer. He moves away from her. "Zeno, take her home. Randy, go with him. If she so much as opens a window, bring her to me."

~26~

Fury and outrage battle inside my chest. I knew getting involved with Tessa wouldn't be easy. I watched her interactions with the Leidolf for far too long, her closeness to them becoming commonplace to the point that I forgot how difficult it was to even get near her when I first moved to town. As public as their clubhouse is, they're always watching Tessa. And not in the same way they watch the other women who work in the Grille. She's different, like a special little pet. Outsiders can walk up to her at the bar, order a drink, and make small talk, but not without one of the Leidolf breathing down their neck. I've seen them insert themselves into her conversations and the ones they don't participate in, they listen to.

And while you might find her outside the Grille, it's unlikely you'll find her alone. One of them is *always* with her. That's why I followed her to the river that night. I couldn't believe she was alone. When she came home with me, I couldn't believe my luck. Tessa is everything I ever thought she would be. Now I just need to get her away from *them*. She doesn't deserve to be caged. She's wild. She's beautiful. And she should be running free.

She should also be eating regularly. It's late, but I follow her home, nodding to the man Zeno when she slides off his bike and runs to me. He doesn't stop me from going inside with her and though she's apologizing for Chopper's actions, what I hear most is the growl of her stomach. My cooking skills are better when I have a full kitchen, but all that's on the menu tonight is boxed spaghetti and jarred sauce. It'll do the trick of feeding us, and Beth.

Waiting for the water to boil, I eavesdrop on the two women's conversation, glad the bikers are staying outside. The eat-in kitchen seats four at the oval table behind me but I don't plan on inviting either of those thugs inside to join us.

The instant Beth sees Tessa's tear-streaked face, she demands to know what happened. The two women sink into opposite seats at the table and start whispering. Tessa's revelations cause Beth's voice to shake. "How would someone other than Gary have that bat?"

Tessa sighs. "Someone must have stolen it."

"But—"

"No!" Tessa shouts. "Gary didn't do it! Someone stole the bat to frame him, and those food service gloves are sold everywhere. Just because they're *like* ones used at the bar doesn't mean they actually came from there."

Beth's nails click over the table. "I never thought Gary could do anything like this either, but I don't understand how some random person snuck into the Grille and made it all the way to his apartment. Who would even try such a thing with all the Leidolf around?"

I dump the pasta into the boiling water and watch Tessa from the corner of my eye. She's tearing the label from her beer bottle, not making eye contact with Beth as she tries to convince herself that someone other than Gary had access to the bat. Beth scoots her chair forward. "Tessa, who would chance stealing from Gary?"

Her shoulders shrug. "I'm still working that part out."

I turn around, wondering if she's going to mention the camera in her office. If her door was open, it has a clear shot of the hallway. "Does Gary not have cameras upstairs? Seems like he'd want cameras everywhere." Her eyes snap up and I lift my shoulders. "I'm just asking, babe."

Beth blows out her breath. "Dad always said Gary had rocks for brains."

Tessa turns on her, her angry face a slab of stone. "It's your *daddy* who has a head full of stones."

Beth is unmoved. "Dad has cameras, and no stranger would walk onto his property and steal anything."

Tessa slides her empty bottle away. "No stranger walked into the bar and got past all the Leidolf either, so like I said, I'm working on the list of suspects, and that list is narrowing."

Beth chews her lip. "You think it was one of Gary's guys, then?"

Tessa gets up from the table and takes plates from a cabinet, not answering the question. Beth looks at me. "*Killing* is *literally* how they got their bad reputation."

Tessa slams the plates onto the table. "They don't murder innocent women!"

Beth folds her hands in her lap. "What if Samantha and Cheryl weren't innocent?"

I grab Tessa's hand and have her hold the colander while I drain the pasta. A safe way to keep her from attacking Beth. "That man, Montrose, he basically threatened to kill you. So why defend them when all Beth is saying is that the easiest answer is usually the right one. The Leidolf are killers, Tessa."

Beth moves to the sink and wraps her arms around Tessa from behind. "The club threatened her?"

"No," Tessa growls, bumping Beth off her without spilling the pasta. "Montrose is one of the few I don't get along with, so he was blowing smoke." She glares at me. "And you saw how the others reacted. Montrose won't touch me."

Beth gets silverware out of a drawer and plops it onto the table. "Still, maybe you shouldn't work in the bar office anymore. Have Matt go with you to get your stuff, and then start working from home."

"Don't you think I'd know if anyone connected to Gary was planning to murder Samantha or Cheryl? The Leidolf are innocent. All of them! And I'm not going to run away like a scared little girl and have everyone in this town saying my actions prove it *is* one of them."

Beth sniffs. "The only thing I know is that Samantha and Cheryl thought they were safe, too. Look what that got them."

I hope Beth's words sink in. Tessa needs to hear this. She needs to let a healthy dose of fear soak into her soul so she'll distance herself from the club. Beth slides a carafe off the counter. "I made us some decaf lattes. Spiked. Because even *I* need a drink tonight."

~27~

Tessa

The smooth click of the front door wakes me. Quiet feet shuffle outside my bedroom door. I rub my eyes, hand searching the empty pillow next to mine. I don't remember much from last night. Matt swirled spaghetti onto my fork and fed me, kissing my sauced lips with a glint in his eye. I vaguely recall being tucked against him as he walked me to the bedroom. My eyes were so heavy I could barely hold them open. He curled up next to me, and I succumbed to the fatigue.

The knob of my bedroom door turns slowly, the wood drifting open to reveal Matt, bare-chested. Getting my eyes to cooperate, I scan the lower half of him. A pair of old blue sweatpants cover his legs. He must have found those in my closet, leftovers from the past that I never got rid of. Warren isn't the first thing I want on my brain when I wake up, and I don't want to see his clothes on my current boyfriend.

Looking away from Matt, I stretch my arms above my head. "What have you been sneaking around doing?"

"Contemplating how beautiful you are in the mornings."

"Only in the mornings?" I wiggle back into the comfort of the warm sheets. "What time is it?"

He crosses to the other side of the bed and slides under the sheets, body scooting over to hold me against the smooth skin of his chest. "You're beautiful every second of the day. And it's still early. Beth needed me to move my car or I wouldn't be out of bed yet."

His lips graze along my neck and I turn my face into the muscle just below his collar bone. I'm not kissing him until I've brushed my teeth. My mouth feels like sewage. "Why is Beth out of bed so early?"

His teeth scrape over my shoulder. "She said she's going by your parents' place before work. Something about the family having a plan to help Gary?"

"They couldn't help themselves out of wet paper bag."

He nips my earlobe. "I can help you out of that shirt."

I move away from him and pull the sheets up to my neck, an ache beginning to thud at the base of my skull. Probably because he's wearing Warren's clothes. "Not right now. I feel like I've been chewed up by a lawn mower."

He leans on the headboard, tucking one arm behind his head and using the other to bring me back to rest against him. "Stress is wearing you down, babe. You went out like a light last night. I barely got a goodnight kiss."

"Sorry. It's just…this situation with Gary is a nightmare."

His thumb kneads the soft flesh of my neck. "You've got a lot on your mind right now. I totally understand that. And I'm here for you. I just need you to give me the chance to be."

I close my eyes, breathe him in, and want nothing more than to stay right here. "Once Gary's out of jail, I'll have more time. Can you wait for me?"

His fingers find my chin and turn me to face him, his blue eyes piercing my heart. "I want to live all your days with you right now, so let me. Especially when they're bad."

"You're the only thing keeping me sane, Matt," I whisper. "But it isn't fair to hold you hostage in this relationship. I know you're upset with me, with the club, and there's not much I can do about rectifying any of what hurts you. But later I can, when all of this is over."

He shifts so that his body is lying next to mine. "Thick or thin, in good times and in bad, I'm here. Because that's what a relationship is, Tessa. This is what *life* is. And I want to spend mine with you." His fingertips glide along my jaw. "I just need you to give me the courtesy of knowing what you're up to. I don't need to be in the secret circle, but I was terrified for a little while yesterday, and then those Leidolf were treating me like some random hookup for you. I didn't like that."

I roll onto my back so I'm not breathing in his face. His breath is minty like he's already brushed. "They're just not used to me having anyone. Outside of them, anyway."

He tugs at the band of the pants he's wearing. "They'll need to get used to me being around then because I care about you. And if you're going to let me stay here, I need to bring some of my clothes over because your stuff is a little small." He moves my hair from my neck and presses his lips to the skin below my ear. "Can I move in with you? I promise to earn my keep by utilizing all the space in this big bed to make your every dream come true."

My stomach quivers, but I smile despite it. "You can move in, but I'm not kissing you until I brush my teeth so cool your jets."

He sits up. "Then go brush because before you get started on this day, I'm going to get started on earning my keep."

~28~

I love every member of Gary's charter. Each man is special to me, and I'm special to them. But even Chopper doesn't love me the way a woman needs to be loved. He isn't interested in settling down, and he's nineteen years my senior. If he wanted a wife or even kids, he'd have them by now. But Chopper chose to shoot blanks long ago. He's dedicated to his brothers and doesn't want anything to distract him from what he feels his purpose is. These past few days, I've been a distraction, and it's making my heart ache.

Then there's Warren. He used me. Wanted everyone *but* me. And he broke me. Now I'm expected to be nice to him. To work side by side with him. To forget about the dark place I was in when he left me, the pit I only climbed out of with Chopper's help. Chopper was there for me, and on the night he first offered to make me forget all my sorrows, he did just that. For a few hours. The next day, nothing had changed between us. Chopper didn't look at me differently or treat me any way he hadn't before. Not after that first time, or the fifth. In my darkness, we'd formed a bond that allowed us to be free with one another.

Matt is like Chopper in that regard. He has a way of taking my mind off things. The difference being that Matt actually wants to love me in all the ways I *need* to be loved. In all the ways that make me feel like it's possible to actually *be* loved. Wholly and completely, and in that forever kind of way. Even this morning, though I know he was upset when I told him I couldn't ride back to the bar with him, he made me a strong pot of coffee and filled my to-go mug, sending me out to Dillon's waiting bike with a kiss that held my mind hostage until I entered the noise of the Grille.

As far as I can tell, no one has an issue with Matt. The club isn't welcoming him with open arms, but they aren't going to accept anyone new right now. Especially with Montrose here. His presence is causing a strain on the club, and I'm fully aware that my actions only add to that strain. But the only thing I respect about Montrose is the patch he wears.

I enter the bar and stroll by him without a word. He will take my silence as disrespectful because there's nothing I can do that he won't consider disrespectful, but I don't know *why* he doesn't like me and I don't really care. Chopper's bike is outside and I need to have a conversation with him.

Chopper isn't downstairs so I climb the stairs to his apartment and barge in without knocking. He's in the bedroom, hair wet, fresh shirt in his hands and jeans hanging low on his hips. A scar reaches out from under his belt loop and slashes upward along his side. He told me it was from a motorcycle accident but it looks more like he had a fight with a knife.

"I'm back," I announce.

He pulls the new shirt over his head and picks up his kutte. "Help run the bar today."

"We have two managers, they'll run the bar."

His icy eyes snap to mine. "Then you can stay here. Don't leave this room."

I pick up a bottle from the side table and throw at his head. He catches it and tosses the unopened beer onto his bed. "Keep the sheets warm for me."

Words choke into my throat. "What is wrong with you? Who *are* you?"

He crosses the floor and stands in front of me. "I have club business to deal with. So stop acting like a child."

"Gary isn't *club business*. He's family! And I'm not the one growling at people and making this situation with Montrose ten times worse!" I take a shaky breath. "Tell me what I can do to help Gary, to help the club, but don't ask me to spend the day locked in your apartment or behind that bar because *neither* of those are going to happen."

He reaches behind me and opens the apartment door. "Go home. Take Matt. And stay there."

Anger slams through me. "Warren is coming here, isn't he?" I check the hallway. "You're bringing him up here." He doesn't answer me. I feel the gates break in my chest, a flood of tears ready to spill, but I'm not going to let him see me cry. "Don't come looking for my help when he crushes you, Chopper. Because he will. You *know* he will."

~

After storming out of the bar, I run to Matt. Falling into his arms reminds me of the days as a kid when I'd run away from home and end up on Warren's doorstep. Because of our parents not getting along, his parents never liked me any more than mine liked him. His mom even threatened to beat me up for sneaking into his room when I was sixteen. Warren had to pin her to the wall to give me time to escape, something he yelled at me for later. He didn't like having to put hands on his mom, but he'd known that she really would have beat me down if she'd gotten her hands on me, so he did it. I never went to his house again after that.

I'm not going to my house like Chopper ordered me to either. I'm going to see Chief, and I'm going to find out for myself what's happening with Gary's case. "Thanks for driving me, Matt. I'm sorry to keep dragging you into this mess."

He gives my knee a squeeze. "We covered this. I *want* to be here for you, so I'm glad you came to me instead of running off alone or asking someone else to bring you to the station. It feels nice being an *us* with you."

I love the sweetness of his dimpled smile. "I'm glad we're together, too. And I'll be even happier once the murderer is caught and Gary is free."

He tugs at the collar of the crisp white button-up he's paired with jeans, the official professional attire of a small town. "Babe, don't get mad when I ask this, okay? Are you sure Gary didn't do it?"

My chest tightens. "Positive."

"What about the bat?"

I shrug. "That's why I need to talk to Gary. Find out who had access to it or if he gave it to anyone."

"Aren't the Leidolf in touch with Gary, though? Surely he's told them his side of things."

I lean my head against the window. "I need to talk to him myself."

Matt pulls into the police station parking lot. "I guess I don't understand why you haven't already. Seems like coming here to beg Chief to let you see Gary is a long shot, and the club claims to already have unfettered access to him..."

I don't want to admit that I'm being frozen out, that Chopper sends me away more than he speaks to me, and that several of the others are no longer making eye contact. It could be because Matt showed up in the bar and had hands on me, which they consider disrespectful to Chopper after the whole growling incident. Or it could be Montrose's influence. He doesn't like that I speak back to him, but if he didn't say stupid things, I wouldn't have to. "There's only so much a person can say on the phone. I want to see Gary face-to-face, and Chief is going to make that happen for me."

Matt sighs. "Gary has a whole life outside of the one you see. What are you going to do if he confesses to you?"

"Gary didn't kill Cheryl! She's his cousin, for crying out loud."

Matt runs a hand down his face. "All I'm saying is people have done a lot worse to their kinfolk, and you seem to live in this bubble where the Leidolf aren't the bad guys their reputation says they are."

"People exaggerate."

He turns in the seat and presses his palm against my chest. "Just promise me you'll consider the evidence, not just this soft heart of yours."

I give him a cold laugh. "You might be the only person around here who thinks my heart is anything but stone."

He smiles. "A privilege I'm happy to have."

"Then let's go in there and get this over with because once Gary is out of jail, I think we should sell my house and choose a new one, together."

His irises blaze. "You're hurting, yet you're considering me? *That's* how I know your heart is gold, Tessa. And I'll work hard to make sure I deserve you every day."

~29~

The instant Chief sees me walk into the station, he comes out of his office shaking his head and repeating *no* like his lips are a broken record. "Now, Chief. You know I need to see Gary and the only way I'm going to get to do that is with your blessing."

His arms cross in a huff. "I just got off the phone with the DA. We've got enough to charge him on Cheryl's case, so outside of his lawyer, no one is getting time with him."

"How are you going to feel about charging him after the real killer strikes again?"

His jaw snaps tight, words coming out between clenched teeth. "I don't want to hear talk about another murder in my town. If Gary is innocent, he can prove it in court."

Matt's fingers tighten on my bicep as he moves in close, his way of asking me to be quiet while he does his own line of questioning. "We heard you found a bloody bat with Gary's fingerprints on it?"

Chief's eyes narrow on him. "I'm not at liberty to discuss the particular evidence in this case."

"Except with Warren?" I counter. "What happened, Chief? He find you in a compromising position with someone?"

Chief's hand snaps forward, fingers tightening on my other bicep with a tug that breaks me out of Matt's grip. Chief rushes me into his office and slams the door in Matt's face. When he reaches for the blinds to close the view from the window that lets him watch over the station, I can't help but lash out. "You sure you want to do that, Chief? I might accuse you of some things, and I'm *real* good at making noise."

"Now you listen here!" He jabs a finger in my face. "We're not dredging up what happened all those years ago just so you can go on some vindictive tirade to clear the name of someone you have a misguided affection for!"

"Is that what your feelings for Erin were? Misguided? Or are those the feelings you have for your wife, and you're too much of a coward to tell her you don't love her?"

Spit draws to the corner of his mouth. "That band of criminals you call family are the only cowards in this town." He throws a hand toward me. "And the only decent one in the lot has the nerve to come in here and *threaten* me?"

"I wouldn't have to threaten you if you'd just let me see Gary. And you can also tell me why Warren all of a sudden has privileges to run amok in this station. Is he snitching for you?"

"I don't believe ninety percent of what Warren says and the other ten percent I know is a lie."

"Then why does his word condemn Gary for Samantha's murder? And why did you let him see a bat that has my name on it without ever even telling me you had it?"

His spine stiffens. "Warren saw the bat? After it was recovered from the scene?"

I shrug. "So he says."

"Damn it to hell!" He storms to the door. "Someone get Rene in here right now!" He slams the door shut. "He's been sniffing around that girl and I told her to keep her distance, but it looks like she decided to let him into our evidence locker instead."

He sits on his desk, arms crossed and glaring at the door. When Rene comes in, she's going to have quite the treat. Especially when she sees me sitting here. She's a year older than me and a full foot taller, but that didn't stop me from blacking her eye when she asked Warren to go to her senior prom. She's avoided me like the plague ever since. "I'll make you a deal, Chief. I get to see Gary, and then I won't sue this department for gross mishandling of the evidence."

~

Getting to stick around for the chewing out that Chief gave Rene was rewarding. It felt good to see her face turn two shades of crimson. She's always been a boy-crazed ditz and Warren used that against her. According to her, they recently bumped into each other at a gas station and had a conversation that ended with him asking her out. They had dinner that night, after which he told her it would be sexy to make out in a police station, the evidence room in particular.

She said Warren didn't touch anything, only looked, but Chief knows better than me how Warren's unauthorized presence could throw off not just Gary's case, but others. The vein in Chief's neck hasn't stopped throbbing since Rene first walked in. He's already fired her, and now that she's reduced to a sniveling pile of sobs, he's no less angry. Mainly because she won't shut up. "I thought it wouldn't hurt to just let him in the side door for a minute."

I sit forward. "There's a side door to the evidence room?"

"No." Chief's voice is hard, eyes cold as he glares at Rene. "She snuck him in a door that no one would be watching at that late hour and took him where he wanted to go because she knows our schedules and how understaffed we'd be when she brought her boyfriend in. Which *proves* you knew what you were doing was wrong, Rene, but you did it anyway."

She wipes her eyes. "I told him we could only do one kiss, and that's all we did. A quick little kiss."

I roll my eyes. "There's nothing little *or* quick about Warren."

Chief shoves back to his feet and motions for Rene to get out of his office. "Go write a statement, and then pack your belongings. I want you out of this building within the hour."

She shuts the door behind her and I prop my elbows on my knees. "So, what happens now?"

He pinches the bridge of his nose. "I told Mayor that I didn't want that boy anywhere near our police vehicles, but he gave Warren the contract anyway, and now people think he's something, let their guards down…" His eyes dart to mine.

"Go on." I prompt. "Tell me how righteous you and all the people who work here are."

His chest puffs. "Erin and I had a consensual *adult* relationship. That's a far cry from armed robbery."

My gut pinches. He could be referring to any number of crimes, many of which track back to someone I'm either related to or friendly with, but I'm certain the one he's referring to is the robbery Warren committed with Jessop. Neither of them faced charges. The guy they tied up and robbed was the store owner and he confessed to hiring Jessop for an inside job. He wanted his liquor store robbed so he could collect insurance money, a plot that might have worked if the man hadn't gotten greedy enough to fabricate his losses to the degree that had red flags racing each other up and down Main Street. Warren left town, and nothing was connecting him to the scene so Chief couldn't arrest him. Jessop *was* arrested but cut a deal for immunity and rolled on the store owner, the fish the prosecutor wanted.

I didn't know about the robbery job until it was done. And I only found out that my dad had been the catalyst, setting the whole plan in motion, after Warren showed up again and my dad came to me, telling me to "Do what you have to do to keep him quiet." At the time, I was in the middle of a heartbreak that had Warren's prints all over it. Dad telling me it would be my fault if Jessop went to jail made it worse. But it was when Dad said he'd never directly talked to the store owner, that it had been

Mom who was the contact, that everything inside me died. If I didn't go to Warren and meet whatever demands he had in order to keep him quiet, my mom's life was on the line. So I didn't go to Warren. I went to Gary, and that night he left me with Chopper.

"Chief, when do I see Gary?"

He jabs a finger against a button on his desk phone and lifts the receiver. "I'll get him out of lockup and give you five minutes with him. Until then, get out of here. And start picking better boyfriends. I like this new one less than the first, and the first one just caused me to have to admit to evidence tampering for every case I'm holding anything for!"

I tread to the door. "I'm not Erin. Even if I break up with Matt, you still don't have a shot."

His notepad slams into the door beside my head. "Get out of here!"

I pick up the notepad and peruse it before I toss it back to him. "Pleasure doing business with you, Chief."

~30~

Sitting in front of Gary is emotional. There's a hardness in his eyes that triggers a fear I shouldn't have. He isn't happy to see me. Like Chopper, he wants me out of his sight. "I'm not afraid of Montrose," I mutter into the handset pressed to my ear. Gary hasn't picked his up. He's only glaring at me through the glass.

"Someone's killing women I love." He doesn't need the phone to be heard. "Where do you think that lands you?"

I raise a shoulder. "No one is dumb enough to mess with me."

His fist lands on the glass in front of my face, blood and spit spraying from where he bit his lip throwing his weight into the punch. "They were there when I dropped Cheryl off! Lying in wait for me to leave so they could gut her ear to ear!" He fights the guards trying to hold him, shouting through the glass. "You're not safe! You're not safe!"

Tears stream down my face. I stare at his blood running down the glass and feel his words vibrate through me, echoing back as the guards overpower him and drag him from view. My body moves of its own accord, feet running, carrying me from the room and straight into Matt's arms.

He holds me tight. "What happened?"

I bury my face in his chest. "Gary doesn't want to see me."

He rubs my back. "Did he say why?"

My fingers drag the fabric of his shirt into my fists. "He thinks I'm next."

His body stiffens. "He said that to you?"

I lift my face from his shirt. "He didn't say it. He *screamed* it. I've never seen him act that way before."

"Geez." Matt tucks me under his arm and begins the trek out of the waiting area. "No one is going to hurt you, okay? I won't let them."

My tears soak patterns into Matt's once crisp shirt. He opens the passenger door of his sedan and attempts to settle me in the seat. The sound of motorcycles roars down the street. Matt goes pale as the club surrounds us. I grip his hand. "Get in the car."

"No. You said Gary just flipped out and—"

I let go of him and move away from his vehicle. "Get in the car, Matt. If they give you an opening, take it. Drive away."

"Tessa—"

"Drive. Away. Go to my house and wait for me."

~

I take the old jewelry box Grandma gave me off my dresser, wiping the dust from the top and opening the scratched yellow box. I hardly wear jewelry, but now I wish I'd done more than just keep Samantha's necklace tucked in this box. There's not much else in it: a few pairs of earrings I got attached to as a teen, a bracelet of plastic beads that Warren gave me, and a fake strand of pearls from my mom.

"What are you doing?" Beth whispers from my doorway. When Chopper dropped me off, she was sitting at the kitchen table with a worried and angry Matt. I was only a few minutes behind Matt, though, so it wasn't long enough for any real panic to set in. Chopper doesn't mince words. I knew quickly what was happening and what few choices I have in the matter.

I set the jewelry box on the bed, closing the old memories off. "Is Matt still upset?"

Her eyebrow raises. "Apparently he cooks when he's pissed, so could you make him mad more often?"

"He's dating me, so him being mad often is a given."

"Good." She grins. "Finish whatever you're doing and get in here. I can tell he's ready to kiss and make up."

"I'll be there in a few."

She leaves and my heart sinks even further. I look around my room. It feels safe enough, especially with Matt and Beth laughing in the kitchen. But Gary doesn't agree. That's why Chopper didn't leave when he dropped me off. He's still outside, and not because he intends to watch my house all night.

When I climbed onto the back of his bike, I could hear Gary's voice belting from the phone pressed to Chopper's ear. The club is tracking me via my phone now, but Randy didn't realize where I was heading after I left the police station until I was nearly at the jail. Not enough time to cut me off, and me showing up in front of Gary let him know that they weren't *handling* me the way he told them to. Per Gary's orders, I'm to pack, get on Chopper's bike, and disappear. Something he ordered days ago, but at that time, he'd given my charge to Zeno, and Chopper didn't want to let me leave his sight. So he broke Gary's order and let me stay, and *that's* why the guys aren't making eye contact. Chopper stuck his neck out for me, and they all have a difference of opinion on why and whether or not he's right. Opinions that no longer matter. The law has been laid down. I'm leaving.

Slipping into the kitchen, I watch Beth smack Matt's hand with a wooden spoon, the two of them in front of their respective pans having an egg cook-off that Matt looks to be winning. "It smells good in here."

Matt turns around, a smile spread across his handsome face. "We're having breakfast for dinner. A birdie told me you *really* like waffles."

I wink at my birdie Beth and fold myself into the crook of Matt's waiting arm, his scrambled eggs light and fluffy while Beth's are thin and overcooked. "I love waffles. They're the perfect vessel for my butter." His eyebrow hikes and I laugh. "I slather my waffles in butter until all the little indentions are filled with sweet cream. I've eaten them that way ever since I was a kid, cutting them into strips and dipping them into just a little bit of syrup."

He kisses the top of my head, pouring his eggs from the pan and onto a waiting platter. "Good thing I make my scrambled eggs with butter."

We move to the table where he already has plates set out. I sit beside him and plop a waffle onto his plate. "Let me show you the proper art of eating a waffle."

The front door busts open, slamming against the doorstop and bouncing back. Chopper's form advances, bypassing the kitchen and heading down the short hallway to my room. Matt drops the silverware onto the table. "What's he doing?"

I lean against the back of my chair. "He's ransacking my closet."

Matt waits for an explanation. I swallow. "It's Gary, he's *ordered* me to leave."

"Leave where?"

I take a breath, watching Beth drop her own fork, the life draining from her face. More than anyone, she knows how close Gary and I are. There was a time when she was jealous of that closeness, feeling as if I didn't care about her as much as I care about Gary. I think that's another reason I let her live with me rent-free, I feel guilty that she's right.

"Gary is scared that I'm being targeted, so he wants me out of town."

Beth gasps. "Being targeted by the serial killer? Why?"

I rub my face, bristling as Chopper's boots stomp into the bathroom, followed by what sounds like him scraping everything off the shelves into a bag. "Gary and the guys are convinced the murders are connected to Gary. *If* that's true, then I could be a target because of my connection."

Matt's arms fold as Chopper storms out of the house, two duffle bags in tow. "Whether or not this has anything to do with Gary, there's a killer on the loose, which is why I've been staying with you. *I'm* the one keeping you safe, not them. And I'm doing it without bossing you around like you're a child."

"He's got a point." Beth swallows, looking over my shoulder as Chopper stomps back into the house. "What about me? Am I in danger?"

Chopper's fingers close around my arm, yanking me from my chair. I understand now that he's been conflicted because of me, bucking his sworn loyalty and despising himself for it. I shake my head at Matt, making sure he doesn't attempt to take Chopper on. I'm not so sure Chopper wouldn't drive a knife through Matt's skull. "Beth's right, Chopper. If someone is after me and they can't get to me, they could go after her. I mean, this little plan Gary hatched isn't going to stop a murderer from murdering, it's only going to change the target. And I don't want to live with anyone else's blood on my hands."

Matt moves to my side. "She also needs to eat. If she wants to go somewhere after dinner, *I'll* take her."

Chopper releases my arm, storms to the refrigerator, throws open the door and stomps back to the table with a stick of butter. He glances at Beth. "Go to your boyfriend's, to work, and back to your boyfriend's." His angry eyes turn on me, hand slamming a stick of butter onto the stack of waffles. "You'll eat on the ride. Now, are you walking out that door or am I carrying you?"

~31~

I haven't seen Matt in forty-eight hours. Though angry with me for leaving with Chopper, he agreed to stay with Beth until she could make arrangements to move in with Arnold—something she's refusing to do. Kind of like how Chopper is refusing to have a separate hotel room. We haven't gone too far from Hinton but each night he's had us in a different location and slept on the floor next to the bed, the two of us existing in near silence.

That first night, I swung on him after he stopped by an old abandoned house and smashed my phone against its stone foundation. All that punch got me was two broken fingers that I then had to endure for three more hours until we got to the hotel he intended to stay at. We checked in and he disappeared, coming back with a baggie of ice and a burner phone. He taped my two fingers to a third, splinting them, and told me to use my elbow next time.

I used the burner phone to text Matt and have been doing so about every hour since. So I'm not surprised that I'm hearing from him now, but this time it's a phone call instead of our usual text. "Hey, handsome."

Matt's breath rolls out of the phone and I close my eyes, remembering the feel of him on my skin. "Did you call just to make me miss you more?"

"Tessa, where are you?" He asks a question he knows I can't answer.

134

I lean against the headboard. "I'm wrapped up in a whole heap of missing you."

A woman's voice trickles over me, muffled in a way that sounds like Matt put his hand over the phone. I sit up. "Is that Beth?"

"Yeah." His voice cracks, the background sounds coming to life once again.

"Where are you?"

More muffled sounds and then his strained voice comes back on the line. "I was driving Beth home from work and we decided to stop and get take-out. When we left the sub place…babe, I thought it was you. Beth freaked out and Chief…"

My blood goes cold. "You thought who was me?"

He sucks in a breath. "There's a body in the middle of the road. I could see her hair and…she looks just like you."

I get off the bed. Panic rising up my throat. I snap at Chopper though I know he's already listening, and I turn on the speaker so he can hear. "What body, Matt? Who is in the middle of the road?"

"I don't know." He sniffs. "Beth said she does."

"Put her on the phone." I wait, pulse pounding in my ears.

"Isabel." Beth sobs. "It's Isabel, Tessa."

Shock rattles through me as Matt and Beth describe what they can see of the scene, the road blocked off and all bystanders being told to stay back. There's a sheet over Isabel's body. A white sheet staining red in an area much too large for her petite frame. Matt heard an EMT say "Another one gutted." While shaking his head at the driver of a different ambulance who'd arrived at the scene.

"Beth said she doesn't know if Gary and this girl knew each other." Matt sniffs. "Do you?"

I shake my head, eyes locked on Chopper's. "Gary doesn't know her." I do. She moved here when I was in ninth grade. She and Beth were the same age but didn't run in the same circles.

One night, I overheard her saying Beth shouldn't be at a party that we were all at. Everyone told her not to mess with Beth or she'd have to deal with me, but Isabel only shrugged, as if she didn't care she'd been overly loud in her judgment of Beth. My sister had heard every word. I tried to get Beth to stay at the party but she wouldn't. After she left, I walked into the party, threw eyes at Isabel's boyfriend—the one she kept telling everyone she was going to marry—and made out with him right in front of her. It was a teachable moment for Isabel. And she did learn. I never heard another bad peep out of her, about anyone. In fact, I almost haven't heard *any* peeps out of her. She became quiet and kept to herself, and these days she only comes back into town to check on her mom who is the only remaining member of her family in Hinton.

I swallow down the memories of Isabel and what I did to her that night. Since Warren jilted me, I understand how badly my actions hurt her. "Matt, take Beth to the Grille. I'll meet you there in an hour."

~

Chopper doesn't fight my decision. He gets on the phone with the club and grabs our bags, securing them on his bike and firing up the beast. My insides churn, twisting and knotting as chaos unfolds inside me. Isabel's death can mean so many things. One being Gary's innocence, another being *my* connection to these last three victims, and the first. Maybe Gary isn't the link. Maybe I am. Maybe all of this is only a coincidence.

I hold Chopper tight and he folds a hand over where mine clasp against his abdomen. There's a killer in Hinton, and he's escalating.

Chopper pulls around to the back of the bar and it hits me that I haven't seen my vehicle in a while. I do go through spells of hardly driving myself anywhere, but at least I usually know where my wheels are. Now, time is passing in weird chunks of days, not hours.

Before we get off the bike, I rest my head on Chopper's shoulder. "The club didn't do this, right? They wouldn't…"

He looks up at the night sky, the stars above us deceptively calm. "We don't kill women."

"I believe you," I whisper. "And I'm sorry that I'm a distraction for you. For Gary. For all the Leidolf."

He removes my hands, keeping hold of one of them as he climbs off the bike. I follow his lead and stand in front of him. He pulls me close and holds me, pressing his cheek against mine. In his way, he's telling me that it's okay, but I still feel horrible.

He slides his hand back into mine and walks toward the Grille, nodding to Zeno as we enter and tightening his grip when Montrose comes into view. The senior man walks toward the sanctuary and Chopper releases my hand. "Go find Beth."

Hurrying by the sanctuary door, I head for the main bar. Matt's waiting for me, worried eyes trained on the hallway. I run to him, tears hot against my cheeks. "It's okay, babe," he whispers against my ear. "It's okay. I've got you."

Beth is behind him, huge red-rimmed eyes trained on my bandaged fingers, mouth twisting in a gasp of words I can't stop from spilling. "What happened to your hand?"

Matt's arms slide from around me and pull my hands into his. Crimson flushes up his neck, curse words flying from his mouth. I press my lips to his. He pulls away. "What did Chopper do to you?"

"Nothing." I sigh. "He just has a hard head."

A snicker draws my attention. Warren is cozy on a nearby barstool, a mug of beer nestled between his palms. I break away from Matt and hit the mug full force. Warren jumps from the stool but not in time, beer splatters his chest like a gunshot wound. "What the hell, Tessa!" he yells.

Matt pulls me backward, tucking me tight against his chest. Montrose's voice bellows from behind me. "Knock it off!"

I smile at Warren. "I just did."

He tugs his faded blue t-shirt over his head and throws it at Beth. "Here. You've always wanted a piece of me."

I lunge for him, doing what Chopper said and throwing an elbow. Matt uses my momentum to spin me around, hard eyes lowering to mine. "Let. It. Go. We've got bigger problems than a fight with your ex."

"Listen to your boyfriend," Montrose spits, glancing at Chopper, who is standing next to him. "Whichever one of them can keep you from causing problems."

~32~

Montrose's words cause Matt to stiffen. Chopper has no reaction, and that's somewhat helpful, but Randy saves the day by locking the front doors and telling everyone to sit down. The club wants Matt and Beth's first-hand account of what happened, and each man listens with intent while they give every detail of what they encountered on the road earlier tonight.

I'm not able to look up from my chipped nails. Matt's voice cracks when he talks about seeing the flashing lights up ahead, stopping behind an ambulance and walking along the side of the road to see what was going on and if he could help. That's when he saw Isabel's hair sticking out from under the sheet. There's mud on the knees of his jeans from where the shock took his legs out from under him.

The room goes still, Beth's soft sobs filling the heavy silence. My chest tightens, the pressure of knowing *I* should be the one to say something closing around my throat. All I can think is that somehow, all of this is my fault. People are dead because of me.

Matt's arm tucks around me, forehead resting against my temple. "I'm so glad it wasn't you."

Montrose tips his stool toward the bar. "Something happens to *her* and we won't have to worry about getting Gary out of jail, he'll tear it down and feed it to us brick by brick."

My eyes snap to his. His leathery face is sullen. Hard. A mix of disdain for having to accept me and agitation over someone killing women right under his nose. He thought he'd come to

139

town and set things right, but there's not a member of the Leidolf who've come up with any real leads. "Have you talked to Gary? Does he know there's been another murder?" My voice comes out weaker than I'd care to have it, but it's either speak softly, or let them hear the guilt that's chewing up my soul.

Randy nods. "I sent the message."

Matt shifts beside me. "I'm going to take Tessa and Beth home."

"Tessa stays." The command comes from Chopper.

Matt's hand tenses on my shoulder. I hear the inhalation and get to my feet, bringing him with me to stop whatever words are wanting to flow from his mouth next, before the men in this room throttle him. "I'll be upstairs. If Gary calls, I want to talk to him."

Attempting to hurry from the bar, Matt in tow, I cringe as Beth comes scrambling into the hallway after us. "Wait! What about me? Do I have to stay here?"

I glance over my shoulder. Chopper shakes his head. I turn back to Beth. "One of the guys will take you wherever you want to go. But you can't be alone. Either go to Arnold's or to Mom's."

Her arms fold, feet clomping along behind us until we reach the bottom of the stairs. "You know I hate riding on their bikes!"

"Then call Arnold," I snap, inner turmoil getting the best of me. "I need Matt right now so please, Beth, find a ride to someplace safe. Now would be a great time for you and Arnold to take that vacation he's been wanting."

Her eyes brim with tears. "I thought *you* were my safe place. And if Matt's with us I don't see why we can't go home. I want to go home!"

I let go of Matt and wrap my arms around her. "I do, too. But I can't. Gary has enough trouble without worrying about me."

Matt brushes the hair from my neck, resting his palm over my sticky flesh. "I'm worried about you, too. I'm worried about you being *here*. You already have a broken hand."

I drag in a breath, leaning away from Beth to slip an arm around his waist. "I cracked a couple of fingers trying to make a point on Chopper's face. And you're getting pretty good at holding me back which is probably why they're letting you stay here with me." I give him a weak smile and tilt my lips to Beth's cheek. "I'm sure you're welcome to stay, too. Gary's apartment is a two-bedroom and it's pretty nice."

She bristles. "I can't be around these hooligans. I swear one of them is the killer. Everyone is saying so."

"Every idiot with a mouth." I groan, pulling free of her. "And you're in their house, be respectful."

Beth scans the hallway, shivering as if she's terrified to be standing inside the Grille. I move away and top the stairs. Matt doesn't follow. I look back at him. "You coming?"

He says something to Beth and then follows me to Gary's apartment, clicking the door shut behind him. "Beth is calling Arnold. I told her to wait inside until he gets here."

"Thanks," I mutter, heading to the kitchen.

He comes up behind me. "She's scared, Tessa. We're both scared. You didn't see what we saw tonight."

I take a glass from the cabinet and go to the sink, fixating on the water lapping up the clear edges. "I'm scared, too. I'm terrified for everyone in this town."

I feel the heat of the tears before I realize I'm crying again. Matt's arms circle me from behind, hands moving to turn the faucet off and set my overfull glass aside. "This is a rough time for all of us. Just…if you don't respect me and my decisions, the Leidolf aren't going to respect me, and I'm tired of them ordering you around like you belong to them. They didn't exactly keep Samantha or Cheryl safe, what makes you think they're going to keep anything from happening to you?"

My head shakes, tears plopping onto the rim of the sink. "I'm not here because I'm too scared to buck the club. I'm not even here because I'm worried I'm next. At this point, let the killer come for me."

His lips fall against my head. "Don't say that."

I shrug. "It's true. Because I think…" I think I'm the cause of this somehow. That my life ending will end the murders. "Matt, I—"

The apartment door swings open. Startled, we both turn around. Warren stops in the archway between the living and dining rooms, t-shirt dangling from his back pocket. His jaw ticks when he sees my tears. "I need to talk to you. Alone."

"No." I sniff.

He takes a step forward. Matt moves from behind me. "She said no."

"She says lots of things," Warren growls.

Matt advances and I slide between them, anger rushing hot and fast. "Stop! I've had enough. I need rest. So *leave*, Warren. Because I'm going to break whatever spell you put on Gary and when I do, you'll beg to be gutted like these women have been."

His expression hardens. "Then what do you think Gary's going to do when he finds out your boyfriend is a cop?"

~33~

Disbelief is easy. It's the knowing that's the problem. In the midst of defending Matt, I caught sight of his face, my own countenance falling with every line of worry tracing across Matt's. Warren isn't lying. Matt's a cop.

Every fiber of my being vibrates, molecules ready to come unglued. "You're using me."

He reaches for me. I retreat. "Babe," he whispers. "I *was* a cop, I'm not anymore."

Warren huffs. "Once a pig, always a pig."

Matt slams into Warren, the two of them falling overtop Gary's polished wood end table. Warren lands a blow against Matt's jaw and Matt counters by bashing Warren's head into the floor. "Stop!" I scream, Matt's shirt ripping under my grasping fingers. Chopper bursts through the door, shoving me aside and wrapping an arm around Matt's neck. He throws his body backward, choking the larger man to get him off Warren.

"Stop." I drop to my knees, pleading with Chopper to let him go. "They got it all out of their system. They're done." I look into Matt's bulging eyes, pain ripping through my chest. "You're done."

Chopper eases up on the choke and Matt rolls away, coughing and rubbing his neck. I close my eyes, willing my tears to stop. Warren hasn't told the Leidolf about Matt, or else Chopper wouldn't have let him go.

"Come on." I tug Matt's arm, urging him off the floor. In the hallway, I press my mouth to his ear. "Don't come back here again. Not even for a cup of coffee."

His hands grip my arms, holding me close, voice hoarse. "I was only a cop for a year." He pulls back, blue eyes looking deep into mine. "Will you please let me explain?"

I remove his touch. "You hid the truth of who you are for a reason."

He scrubs his hands down his face, jaw already beginning to swell. "Who I *was*, Tessa. Past tense. That part of my life ended three years before I even moved here." He leans his head against the wall, whispering. "I'm not undercover and trying to run a scam on you. Warren is, though. Why do you think he's digging into my past and inserting himself in every inkling of a connection to you?"

I glance to the open doorway, the hushed tones of Warren's voice wafting out. He's definitely up to something, but he isn't wrong for outing Matt. And if he wanted to get rid of Matt, he would have done it in front of the club.

I level my gaze on Matt. "I'll walk you out."

~

Warren and Chopper look up from their respective places in the living room when I reenter Gary's apartment. Warren, still shirtless, stretches his arm along the back of the couch. "Where is he?"

My eyes dart to Chopper's chair, then back to Warren. "Can we talk?"

He swipes his t-shirt from the floor where it pulled from his back pocket in the tussle. He tosses it at me. "I've said all I need to say. I expect you to handle that situation, and wash my shirt."

I ball up the shirt and throw it at his head. "Why are you here? Can't stand to see me happy? You have to barge in and ruin everything about my life all over again?"

"Me?" He climbs to his feet, towering over me. "Sweetheart, you're the one who ruins every relationship *I* get into so don't go putting your jealous tendencies on me. I've stayed out of your life the way you wanted me to. Until now. When a killer is mutilating women and leaving them in our streets." His chest presses into me, face lowering, chiseled jaw hardening with every breath. "I don't care about your *feelings*. I care that there's still breath in your body. *That's* why I'm here."

Chopper raps his knuckles over the table. "Sit down. Both of you."

Warren moves back to his place on the couch and I sit on the opposite arm, not willing to sit next to him. I don't trust for a second that he's here on my behalf, and he's not keeping Matt's secret out of the goodness of his heart. He's keeping that ace up his sleeve for a reason, and will play the card when it suits him best. There's nothing I hate worse than someone having something to hold over me.

Chopper doesn't seem to care what Matt and Warren were fighting about, and he's not interested in any more drama from Warren and me. His face is solemn, which is better than murderous. "Gary called. He still wants you tucked away."

I fold my arms. "Did you tell him I'm not going anywhere? Especially when he won't talk to me?"

He nods. I drop my arms. "Gary has to realize what Isabel's death means. He has absolutely no connection to her."

"You do." Warren's eyes float to mine. "You've got connections to all of them, Tessa. Every single one of them, starting with Layla."

The air around me is heavy, like concrete being mixed into the atmosphere, painful chunks slicing through my lungs as I breathe. My vision grows dark, pulse racing as Warren's voice drones on. The woman murdered the year after Layla was the substitute art teacher I had for three months. The sunny woman with a face as round as her body had more talent in her toenail than I had in the whole of my being. Yet she favored my sketches, hanging them in the hallway and praising the work to anyone who happened by. She was murdered exactly one year after Layla.

The next year it was the sweet lady who worked in the produce department at Foodville. My whole senior year, I'd go in there and buy a fruit bowl before school. When she found out I didn't like cantaloupe, she started making me special bowls with extra strawberries in place of the cantaloupe. Last I heard, she'd retired and moved away to be near her son.

"Last year it was our old high school cook." Warren continues with a heavy undertone of pity. "You're the only one Arlene ever gave graduation gifts to. Heck, you're the only one she ever bothered to come to graduation for."

I slide off the arm of the couch, air no longer willing to penetrate the thick walls of my lungs. Warren sinks into the floor with me, snapping at Chopper to get me some water. "She's having a panic attack."

I dig my nails into the muscles stretching out of Warren's jeans and over his hips. "Air."

His palms rest against my cheeks. "It's all around you. You're okay, just breathe." He mimics the motion, urging me to follow his breathing. "There you go. All you've got to do is breathe. And wash my shirt." I dig my nails into him harder and he laughs, taking the glass from Chopper and bringing it to my lips. "She's going to be just fine."

~34~

Head woozy, the dull throb of an incoming migraine tensing my jaw, I manage to pull myself onto the couch, accepting as little aide from Warren as possible. He sits beside me, rubbing my back. "I haven't told the others about your connection, only Chopper. And Gary."

I move too fast, vision blinking dark and then back to way too bright as I round on him. "What do you mean you told Gary? You think I killed these people?"

He glares at me. "Yeah, I think you strapped on a piece and used your charming personality to get their defenses down so you could gut them while raping them." My face pales and he blows out a breath. "Of course I don't think you killed them. You're not strong enough to move the bodies and…"

He hesitates, glancing at Chopper. I grab his chin and turn him back to me. "And what?"

He knocks my hand from his face. "Before you got Rene fired, I was able to see some of Samantha's file. The guy who attacked her used a condom. He…wasn't gentle during any part of what he did to her."

I understand his meaning. The attack that we think was brutal, it was worse. "Gary knows all of this?" I whisper.

Warren waits for me to make eye contact. "*Everything* I know about the murders, he and Chopper know."

My throat still feels tight. "I'm not the only person who knew these people. Everyone in town knew them. You included."

He shrugs. "Knowing people and having a connection are two different things."

"I wasn't connected to Layla."

He leans his elbows onto his knees, blood smeared along his side from my nails. "You're one of the few people in this town who treated Layla like a person who mattered."

"She did matter."

He smiles. "That's why your connection to her will always be more than everyone else's. You *saw* her, and she saw you. There was a genuineness between the two of you."

"And the woman from tonight?" Chopper asks.

Warren gets up from the couch and goes to the kitchen, opening the refrigerator, pulling out a beer and downing it before answering. "They were friends. Then Tessa made out with Isabel's boyfriend, right in front of me *and* Isabel. We're talking fully clothed sex. That pretty much sealed their friendship."

He chugs another beer and I rub my temples. I forgot Warren had been there that night. He'd been so mad that he'd left the party and wouldn't speak to me for a month. Once he did, it was only to tell me we'd broken up. I took the opportunity to inform him he'd never asked me to be his girlfriend to begin with.

"Doesn't sound like I'm the one who needs to be locked away and guarded by the Leidolf, it's the rest of you who should run and hide. Leave the town to me and the person killing on my behalf."

Warren drops a beer onto the table in front of him, handing another to Chopper. "The women around you sure need to watch their backs, Tess. Except Beth. I say we put her in the middle of Main Street and see who comes for her."

Anger surges forth, driving me to my feet. My already damaged hand shoots forward, coming to an abrupt, hang-in-the-air stop, my arm suddenly heavier than a waterlogged board. I lower it. "We've got to get her back here." I turn to Chopper.

"*If* any of these killings have something to do with me, Beth will be target number one."

He sighs. "I've got Bear on her already. He followed her to your dad's place. Looks like she's staying there for the night. Should be fine."

I lower myself back to the couch. She was supposed to be going to Arnold's. "Bear? Did you tell him my father is an idiot? One who might be pulling strings to get someone else to kill for him?"

Warren leans back and kicks his feet up onto the table. "Your dad is one of the people we've ruled out. He doesn't have the guts to even hire someone to kill."

Chopper nods. "Cheryl's ex is out, too."

I glance at Warren for clarification since he's apparently in the know and Chopper would rather not have to speak. "Gary's locked up with the deadbeat. After he robbed Cheryl, he went and robbed his grandma, stealing her car to jet out of town. He didn't realize that fancy new car of hers had a system that wouldn't only track it, but would shut it off. He's been locked up since before Samantha."

I bite the inside of my cheek, jealous all over again that Warren gets to talk to Gary while I'm iced out. "You sure seem to know a whole lot about this case, and you know all these women. What's *your* alibi, Warren?"

He takes a swig of beer, a glint in his eyes as he lowers the bottle from his lips. "Mostly, I've been checking into the cops around here. One in particular."

~35~

The good thing about living in a bar is that you can always drink yourself numb when you can't sleep. That's what I did earlier, listening to Warren and Chopper whisper about this theory or that, naming names and sorting between themselves what they knew about the person as if they're going to sit in Gary's apartment and solve a murder spree. Every time Warren went on a diatribe about how a man was connected to me or would know about my interactions with the victims from those bygone years, I'd feel sick all over again. A few sounded plausible, others ridiculous.

My elementary school bus driver *did* sometimes bring me cookies and slip them to me as I passed by his seat. But not because he was creepy. He did it to entice me onto his bus because sometimes I'd just sit at the bus stop and watch him drive away, skipping school from the ripe old age of six in favor of going down to the river to catch crawdads. He was old then, and he's practically ancient now, already having walked with a cane by the time Layla was murdered. Last I saw him outside his son's house, he was using a walker.

The postman who used to drive a little too slowly whenever I'd happen by wherever he was delivering *was* creepy. He'd sometimes offer to give me a ride. I'd always decline. Warren tried to fight him once when he saw the man taking pictures of me as I walked away. Years later, the postman was arrested for possession of child pornography but only received probation. He moved to Buchanon the following year but is still frequently in town visiting parents who never believed their son was guilty of anything. They'd tell anyone who would listen that their son was being framed. It didn't take long for people to stop listening. It took even less time for people to just avoid talking about the case altogether. Seems when things make us uncomfortable, we just stick our heads in the sand and avoid them.

As much as I'd love to see the postman behind bars, not believing for a second that people like him can be reformed, the murder victims are outside what I believe his age range to be. If it *is* him, the killings definitely have nothing to do with me. He wouldn't know about my interactions with everyone. He couldn't.

Unsure and uneasy, I slip out of the bedroom where the sheets still smell like Gary. It was fine when I passed out earlier, but waking up surrounded by the reminder that he's gone and unwilling to speak to me for reasons I can't control, I head to the apartment door and open it as quietly as possible. Tiptoeing down the hall past Chopper's room, I move quietly down the stairs and out the back door. Zeno is there, along with several others. They watch me cross the parking lot. My heart pounds as I dip behind the rhododendron and head for Matt's back door. Their boots move across the pavement and I start to knock. Heavy footfall closes in and I pound my fist on the steel slab. It swings open and I rush in inside, pushing Matt back as I close the door.

His tentative hands rest on my shoulders. "Are you okay?"

I face him. All he has on is boxers. A groan rattles through my chest. I want him.

He follows me to his room where I sit on the bed, attempting to separate my real desires from the ones the alcohol is whispering. He sits beside me, taking my hands in his. "Is this about the cop thing, or did something else happen?"

I stare at our hands. "The guys will be guarding your front door by now."

He nods. "I expected as much, but you're not their prisoner. If you want to go home or anywhere else, I'll take you. We'll get by them even if I have to call the cops to do so."

I meet his eyes. He grimaces. "I wouldn't call them because I'm tight with them, I'd call because you're not going to be held against your will and I'm not able to fight our way out by myself." He releases one hand, bringing his fingers to wipe my now falling tears. "If you run really fast, I can stall the men outside long enough for you to escape. No cops. Just me. The man who *really* hopes he still has a girlfriend."

I thought I came here to talk but I didn't. Cop or not, I love Matt. I want to be with him. I press my lips to his. He receives the kiss. "I love you, Tessa."

I climb onto his lap. "I love you, too."

~

Lying on Matt's chest, the steady beat of his heart under my ear, I long to wake up to him every morning. To sip on coffee while he makes waffles for our children. To have them help me decorate his birthday cake year after year, making memories that will outlast us as our family multiplies and grows until Matt and I are just stories told on the lips of generations we'll never meet. "I love you," I whisper.

His fingers tighten on my shoulder. "I love you, too. Thank you for understanding that I can't do anything about my past. I left the force after only a year. It just…wasn't for me. Not that insurance is my dream either. But it brought me here to this town, to you, so all things considered, taking this job was the best decision of my life."

I sit up, knots forming in my stomach. "You swear you're not still a cop? You're not using me to spy on the club?"

He slides himself up in the bed. "Right after I started working patrol, I got a call that a kid was threatening to kill himself. He was fifteen and had gotten into a fight with his girlfriend. His mom called the police and I was the closest. I got there and was talking him down, then the girlfriend showed up, running into the house screaming. She wanted to help him, but in that split second where I turned away from him to tell her to stay back, he pulled the trigger."

I gasp and he winces. "I…couldn't get past that. I'd been on other calls, where the people were already gone before I got there. This one was different."

I wrap my arms around him. "I'm so sorry, Matt."

He holds me tight, face resting in the crook of my neck. "Like I said, all things considered, it's the road that led me to you."

I close my eyes. "When Gary's out of jail, I'll talk to him about you. Until then, you can't be inside the bar. But inside the bar is where I *have* to be."

"Why? Do you not trust that I can protect you?"

I laugh as he makes his pecs bounce. "I'm sure you could fight off Hercules, but Chief isn't speaking to me and the guys are the next best source of information. I'm going to stay with them so I know what's happening, I just want to make sure the distance doesn't hurt us."

He tucks a hand behind his head. "Am I only going to see you at night? Because yeah, that's going to hurt. I want a whole relationship, not just a warm bed at night."

I climb onto his lap. "You're going to have to take what you can get, and I'll make it worth your while." His body responds to me. Satisfied he isn't going to put up too much resistance, I climb off his lap. "Prop your door open for me tonight."

He rubs his face. "Fine."

I press a kiss to his lips. "Can you keep in touch with Beth for me, too? Check on her, make sure she's okay at my parents' place?"

He shrugs. "Sure, but I know she'd rather you be the one checking on her. It's clear that she looks up to you."

I sigh. "In some things maybe, but mostly she's just…wired to overcomplicate things. If I call her, she'll go on a tirade about how bad things are even if they're fine. Still, I'll call and check in with her every day, but the club is keeping eyes on her and I know they freak her out. If, sometimes, I could tell them she's with you and they can back off, that will give her a break and she'll be less prone to calling me every fifteen minutes."

His hands slide to my hips. "So now you want me to babysit for you? That's going to cost you."

I place a final kiss on his lips. "I'll pay you tonight when I come to warm your bed. And I'll also see if I can persuade Chopper to let us go somewhere for lunch later. Just the two of us."

He pulls himself out of bed and lumbers toward the back door, pushing it open to find Rick pressed against the wall. "I'm taking her to lunch later and *none* of you are following us. Get that straight with your *boys* because she's *not* your property." I shake my head as I walk by him and he shrugs. "I don't take orders from anyone, and neither does my girlfriend. I'll check on Beth and be back to get you in three hours."

~36~

It's sweet that Matt wants to stand up for me, but stupid that he's doing it against the Leidolf. Rick didn't say anything as he escorted me back to the building, but I know he'll repeat Matt's words to the others.

Slipping back into Gary's apartment, I click the door shut and rest my forehead against the grainy slab. If Matt would have talked to me his first day in town, we'd be together and happy right now.

"Been with the cop?" Warren's voice slithers from behind me, cutting off my air supply. Lifting from the door, I turn slowly. Warren is sprawled on the couch, a sheet pulled over him.

My jaw clenches. "Did you sleep here last night?"

He nods. "Unlike you. I assume your late-night vanishing act was you doing your job and handling things with the pig?"

I move past him and pull a bottle of Tennessee Honey from Gary's cabinet. I'm going to need this whole bottle of Jack Daniels if I'm going to have to deal with Warren all day. "When I figure out what's getting you a seat at Gary's table, it'll be you I handle. Until then, feel free to jump off the roof. The pavement is nice and hard on the east side."

He gets off the couch and snatches the bottle of Jack as I head for Gary's bedroom. "You go right ahead and find out why I'm here, *babe.* Then you can stop drinking yourself into a stupor that has you sneaking out in the middle of the night to screw cops."

I slap him. He lowers his head, dipping into my face until our eyelashes bump when I blink. "You're going to get him killed. And the more you're with him, the more likely they are to kill you, too. So end it, Tessa. Or *I'll* end it."

I step away from him, anger pushing tears to my eyes. "He's not a cop anymore. He's just someone who loves me, and you can't stand to see me happy."

His mouth twists in disgust and he tosses the bottle to the couch. "I know what the pig's record is. He couldn't hack it as a cop so he bailed, got himself a pencil-pushing job." The cords of his arms flex. "My sources are good, but no one is perfect, Matt could be undercover, working a long angle. But even if he's not, to the club, once a cop, always a cop."

I lift my chin. "When Gary's out, I'm going to talk to him about Matt's past. He'll interrogate Matt, who has nothing to hide, and everything will be fine."

He points at me. "You're a lot of things, but naive isn't one of them. Stop listening to the fantasy being oinked in your ear and get your head straight."

I march to the couch and grab my bottle. "When Gary's out of jail and you're beat to a pulp, you'll see *I'm* not the one living in fantasy land."

His hand crushes mine against the bottle, nostrils flaring as he lowers into my face once again. "I'll be right here when Gary comes home. Now go take a shower, we've got work to do and you smell like pig."

Jerking my hand out from under his, I flip him off and storm into the bathroom, turning the shower on before he hears the explosion of emotions. I hate him. I don't want to be anywhere near him. And I despise knowing he's right. I'm leading Matt into danger. The club *will* associate with cops, but only those who are upfront about it. Matt's been lurking around for years, never a peep about his former profession. And the location of his office…if he was undercover, he'd be in the perfect spot.

~

Hair wet, face scrubbed, eyes puffy, I wrap a towel around myself and tread to the kitchen. Warren and Chopper are sitting at the table. I take a glass and the bottle of Jack out of the cabinet, happy to see Warren had the good sense to put it back up. "I plan to drink this whole bottle, but I'll share a shot if you want one, Chopper."

He doesn't answer. I glance over my shoulder. Warren's narrowed eyes are fixed on me. He'll be less aggressive with Chopper in the room. I make a face and turn back to my drink. "It isn't polite to stare at women. Didn't your wench of a mother ever teach you that?"

He lets out a humorless laugh. "Nope. And there's nothing under that towel Chopper and I both haven't seen so feel free to drop it, our eyes won't bug out."

I grip the glass, turning to face Chopper. His eyes are on the table. I glance at Warren. He smirks. "He didn't have to tell me, I *saw* you together." Blood drains into my feet. Warren looks away. "You're not as smart as you think you are, Tessa. Now if you can manage to get dressed while being drunk, go put on some clothes and help us go through this list Gary gave us."

I pull out a chair at the table, spin and straddle it. Warren tries not to look but color flushes up his neck. I plop my bottle onto the table, draining my glass and filling it again. "What list?"

"The bat with your initials on it is the best lead. Gary knows it was in his room a week before he was arrested because he showed it to someone."

I drain my second glass. "Who?"

Warren's eyes meet mine. "Me."

My bravado sinks into the floor, leaving behind the raw realization that sitting here half-naked and sprawled open only hurts me. I get up from the table, the burn of Warren's eyes worse than the alcohol sliding down my throat. Putting one foot in front of the other, I leave the kitchen and slip into Gary's spare room where I have a clothing stash. The bed is unmade. The bed I've slept in numerous times. The sheet Warren had wrapped around him earlier came from here. He's made himself at home. And has been visiting Gary here without my knowledge.

Dressed, hair left wet to dry in whatever frizzy state of wavy curls it wants to go in because I'm too dazed to care, I go back to the kitchen and sit in the chair next to Chopper. He has a list of names in front of him, some already marked off and others circled. I pull it toward me. "Are these the people who have been in this apartment since the bat was last seen?"

He nods. "The club is still working the angle that the murders are an attack on us."

"But Isabel doesn't fit."

He slides his hand onto my knee. "It does if it was only to draw you back out."

I press my face into the table. I want all of this to stop. "Why can't we find who's doing this? It's one man. Why can't we find him?"

"We're going to, Tessa," Warren assures. "The club is working their angle and I'm working mine. Chopper and Gary are filtering information for both and seeing what fits. We're going to get this guy, it's just a matter of time. And that time would go faster if we didn't have to chase you all over the countryside. Stay where you're told to stay."

I leave the table and grab a pen from a drawer, coming back and sliding the list from in front of Chopper. I print Warren's name at the very top and then slide the list back to Chopper. "He confesses to being the last person to see the bat, he's inserting himself into the investigation, going so far as to break into the evidence room, and he came up with the theory that these murders have something to do with me, giving all sorts of fanciful reasons for that theory." I press my palms on the table and look at Warren. "If there's one person in my life who would know all the tiny connections I have to these women, it's you."

He tilts his chair up on two legs. "This is why you shouldn't drink. Your mouth takes big enough dumps when it's sober, you're a hole in the ground when drunk."

I slam my foot into a lifted chair leg, sending him bouncing off the hardwood. I fake shock, placing a hand over my heart. "Did I do that? Sorry, I must be drunk."

He picks himself up off the floor, rubbing his elbow and sliding the bottle of Jack across the table. "Here. My wench of a mother liked this stuff, too. I always knew you two didn't get along because you were just alike."

Chopper slams a hand on the table to shut us up and answers his ringing phone. "Yeah." His eyes snap to mine and he clicks the phone off. "Chief is downstairs. Wants to talk to you."

Warren makes an oinking sound. "The piggies sure do love you, or is it the other way around?"

Chopper looks between us, questioning. I walk toward the door. "Tell Gary I'm back in with Chief and that I'm coming to the jail again if he won't get on the phone with me. I need to talk to him. Today."

~37~

Chief is waiting for me just inside the door to the Grille. He's watching the crowd, nodding to any townsfolk who pass by either on their way to eat or to leave after having had their fill. He swallows when he sees me and my gut pinches—whatever he's here for, it isn't going to be good.

I'd invite Chief into my office for this private conversation but with the club on high alert, it's best we go outside. "Follow me." I walk by him, out the door and past Brian, taking Chief around the side of the building opposite where the alleyway to the parking lot is. The rhododendrons are thick here, and the only windows are on the second story where the apartments are. I stop beside the outside unit for one of the heat pumps. "Sorry for the cloak-and-dagger but the guys are fidgety."

He hooks his thumbs behind his belt. "I felt that when I walked in. They treating you alright?"

"About as good as I'm treating them."

He nods. "And Beth? How's she after the other night? Deputy Cornwell said she was in a bad way."

I lean on the exposed cinderblock the building was made from. "She and Matt both are bound to have nightmares for a long while. They didn't have to see what you and yours saw, though. How are all of you holding up?"

He looks at the ground, head shaking as his eyes come back to mine. "In all my years, I never thought I'd have to face

160

anything like this. That's why what I'm getting ready to tell you is so hard, but I need you to back me."

The bottom drops out of my stomach. I remain silent, watching the sweat bead on his brow and roll down the side of his face. His collar is already soaked, and it isn't from the heat of the day, humid as it is. He clears his throat and starts slow. "This last murder, it doesn't clear Gary of the others so I can't let him out. The evidence still points to him, especially on Cheryl, and half the town has already tried and convicted him. They'd riot if I release him."

I jerk a thumb to the wall I'm leaning on. "What do you think they're going to do if you don't?"

His face reddens. "I'm hoping you'll talk sense into them. This town has enough problems without them running around here acting like every man walking his dog down the street is a murderer."

"How do you know they're not?"

His teeth clench. "You know I don't believe Gary is capable of this any more than you do, but the evidence is saying something else and I *have* to follow it because someone is out there dropping dead women all over my town."

I push off the wall. "I'm sorry that's such a problem for you, but I'm sorrier for the women being killed left and right while you do nothing but keep an innocent man locked up because it looks good for your public relations."

He paces away from me, catching sight of Brian leaning on the corner of the building before pacing back again. "My hands are tied when it comes to your cousin. The DA is all over him and if they don't nail him for murder, it'll be something else."

"Unless he rolls on someone bigger."

He shrugs. "That's how they like to play the game, but it's Gary's choice to go along with it or not. And it's your choice on how this town handles the situation we're in."

My eyes widen. "So you lock up an innocent man to save face and it blows back in *your* face when the murders don't stop, and now *I'm* the one who is supposed to keep peace in *your* town?"

His Adam's apple bobs. "People around here respect you. You've always been a straight shooter, and even with the deck stacked against you, you land on your feet. That kind of grit is hard to come by, but we all know it when we see it."

I shake my head. "Fluffing me up like that means you're getting ready to ask for something big, and unless part of that deal includes Gary walking free, it's a *heck* no, Chief."

A vein bulges at his temple. "I was hoping you'd see the sense in what the mayor is announcing at a press conference in an hour."

"You got me curious. Spill."

His jaw works, as if pumping itself up to utter whatever words he came here to say. "We're imposing a curfew. Eight p.m. to six a.m. no women are allowed out."

The curse above me registers before Chief's words do. I look up. The window in the spare apartment behind Gary's is open. *Warren. The little eavesdropping rat.* "I'll be back in a minute."

Chief grabs my arm. "I don't have a minute. Just tell me I can count on your support. I'd like to take you with me, have you stand with Mayor and me on the courthouse steps when the announcement is made."

His syllables slowly filter through the sieve of my mind, past the anger and grief, slipping below the sorrow and heartache to rest upon untamed rage. I rip my flesh from his touch. "Are you kidding me?"

"Do you see me laughing?"

"Women," I snap. "You're putting a curfew on *women*. The victims! Put a curfew on men! They're the ones who can't be trusted. They're the ones *murdering* people!"

It's no secret that I have a tendency to raise my voice and I know Matt's keeping a close eye on the Grille, watching for me to step out of the building, but I'm still marginally surprised that he's popping around the corner, shouldering past Chief to fall into place at my side. "What's going on, Chief Dunbar? You can't harass Tessa, and this is hardly an appropriate place to question someone."

Chief jabs a finger at him. "I'm not harassing anyone and a punk like you will never have enough starched white shirts to run this town, so you drop the attitude when you speak to me."

I shove Matt behind me, wondering why Brian let him pass. "Maybe it's a punk like Matt who *should* be running this town because all you and the mayor have managed to do is let a killer run free through the streets. *No*, Chief, I will *not* stand on the steps with you. I'll be at the bottom of them, with every woman in this town, calling for your head."

~38~

Brian's behavior toward Matt is tickling a suspicion but I don't have time to contemplate the actions of the wolves right now. And even if they are genuinely giving Matt a pass on my behalf, I can't let Matt back into the bar yet so I send him to his office and go to the sanctuary with Brian to fill the club in on what Chief is up to. As my words spill, a tension builds that makes the hair on my arms stand up and the back of my neck prick.

"I'm not going to let this stand." I finish. "We're not turning back time and oppressing women simply because men are idiots."

Chopper nods. "Go do what you've got to do."

I turn on my heel and leave the sanctuary. None of the guys follow me so I text Matt and ask him if he can drive me to city hall. He responds that he'll be waiting out front and I make my way into the Grille, eyes landing on Warren. He's hunched over a table in a dark corner with his phone pressed to his ear. I step behind the bar, pour a beer, stride over to him and dump the foaming mug straight over his head.

While he bellyaches, I walk out the front door and get into Matt's waiting car. As we pull away, Warren races outside, beer dripping from his nose. And now Matt's upset with me. Somehow he thinks any attention I give Warren diminishes Matt's place in my life. I maintain that my interactions with Warren have nothing to do with Matt. "I want Warren out of my life, and I'm going to mistreat him until he is. Simple as that."

"Nothing is ever that simple, Tessa."

I shrug. "Just you watch and see."

An odd feeling sweeps through me as Matt drives us to pick up Beth. No Leidolf are following us. I look at the phone Chopper gave me. It's probably being tracked but it still doesn't make sense that I'm suddenly allowed to just walk away from the club. "You expecting a call?" Matt asks. "Maybe a simple text from an ex you claim to not have feelings for?"

I open a social media app. "Nope, just contemplating how best to blow up Mayor's announcement."

Beth bounds our way and gets in the backseat, announcing she's already called Marla and some of her other friends. "Word about the curfew is spreading as we speak."

Matt groans. "You two are the perfect pair."

"We're sisters." I wink at Beth and give Matt a smile. "Next stop is city hall."

Fights with Matt are benign. He doesn't say another word about my *attention* giving while Beth and I burn up the phone lines, asking everyone, not only women, to march on city hall. By the time we enter Main Street it already looks like parade day. People line both sides of the street waving anything they have in their hands. Some even have signs that read *Thou Shall Not*, a true mark of being in the Bible Belt. We'll fill in the rest of the sentence with any old thing we like: kill, steal, imprison women…as long as it's doused by the Old Testament tongue it's bound to be blessed and presumed to be right.

Finding a metered parking spot in front of one of the two law offices in this town, Matt pulls to a stop and begins searching for change. "Leave it." I laugh. "They don't have the manpower to bother with tickets today. They're going to be too busy keeping us off their precious steps."

The assembled crowd isn't proof that Chief has it right about me. I don't hold any kind of power of persuasion over this town. I'd argue I have the opposite. But the people around me are here today because despite our backward reputation, common sense is common any way you spin it. To force women from the routine of their lives, telling them they can't leave their homes after dark or drop their children off at a sitter's early enough to be on time for work is akin to telling a dog it can't bark because someone might kick it. If a dog gets kicked, it's the owner of the foot who is at fault.

I march to the front of the crowd gathered at the bottom of the courthouse steps, where a red velvet rope from the theater down the street is being used to block off the concrete stairs. Chief and I lock eyes. I delivered on my promise and he's livid. His hand moves to the shoulder of the officer next to him, mouth pressing close to the man's ear. Brady's eyes bounce over the crowd, landing on me. I wave at him. He waves back, earning himself an unfriendly backslap from Chief. Brady is a few years older than Beth. She used to have a huge crush on him, then he asked out her former best friend and well, that's how they became former friends.

Beth tugs my sleeve. "Did Brady just wave at me? Oh no, please tell me he isn't flirting at a time like this! Who does that? And his wife is prego, the size of two houses glued together with bowling balls!"

"I think he was telling me he's meant to keep an eye on me, but it isn't *me* he has to worry about." Satisfaction wells up inside me as the thunderous roar of motorcycles vibrates the ground we stand on. I watch Chief turn his attention to the noise, bike after bike parading past us, encircling the buildings of city hall. The club isn't abandoning me. They've been waiting for me to get here.

Murmurings stir the crowd. Some people think the club is here to keep the peace, others believe there will be a shoot-out, police against bikers and innocent casualties caught in the crossfire. I stand my ground as the people begin to inch away, clearing space for a brawl if one does break out.

Mayor takes his place behind the podium. A hush settles over the square as his words begin to waft from the scratchy speakers sitting off-center on either side of him. "Our town is facing unprecedented times. Our lives, namely the lives of the women and young ladies we hold so dear, are being threatened by a predator we've never encountered before. While our own police force, led by Chief Dunbar, works around the clock, utilizing resources from the state police, FBI, and multiple law enforcement agencies in neighboring towns and cities, there can be no mistake made about the necessity of having each and every citizen of Hinton involved in bringing the murderer, or *murderers*, to justice."

His emphasis on *murderers* is directed at me, his way of letting me know that they have no intention of letting Gary off the hook. Mayor's jab backfires, though. The thought of multiple killers has crossed everyone's mind but hearing it from the mayor's mouth makes it real. He puts his hands in the air to deflect the shouted questions, the accusations, the necessary panic that he's trying to play off as uncalled for. "As all of you well know, we have someone in custody—" More shouts, this time accompanied by the roar of bikes. The club is making its statement, and Mayor is backpedaling.

Chief trains his eyes on me and I return the favor, the two of us stuck in a staring match as Mayor continues his speech. "As I was saying, we are working tirelessly to bring the murderer to justice." His voice echoes across the pavement and concrete, over the decorative shrubs wilting in the heat of a hot July sun. The crowd settles down and Chief's lip ticks up. I narrow my eyes. The club won that battle, publicly taking Gary off the suspect list.

"Today," Mayor continues, "I stand before you with a heavy heart for those we've lost. I stand before you mourning with their families, folks who, like me, will never understand why their loved one was taken from them, and in such a brutal way. I stand before you as *one* man, and I ask the good people who made this one man your mayor to please help us. We can't lose another girl. The Bible tells us to love and protect our women, for her price is *far* above rubies. As the one man that I am, with a mother, a wife, daughters, daughters-in-law and granddaughters, I can affirm that the Bible is correct in that there is no greater treasure in my life than the very existence of the women who surround me day in and day out."

He reaches a hand toward his wife, who dutifully steps forward, slipping her palm into his while simultaneously lifting a tissue to her eye with the other. "I've had to make a tough call today. One that many of you may not like. But as my God-given directive to keep the women around me safe, and because of the duties I embrace as they were placed upon me by the hardworking citizens of this town, I will *not* cower from my responsibilities or take a single day off from doing what the good Lord placed upon me as a man to do. Effective immediately, the town of Hinton is under curfew for all women, of any age, between the hours of eight p.m. and six a.m." He waits for the crowd's response, a mix of shouting and cheers.

Cheers. Applause. Celebration. It all grows, building slowly around me until the lambs in the group fall in line and cheer with their peers. Chief hooks his thumbs through his belt, victorious in his coaching of Mayor. Chief knows how to pull this town onto his side and he does it with the Bible. "Thou shall *not* punish women for the sins of men!" I shout, ducking under the rope and climbing the stairs. "Thou shall *not* victimize the *victims!*"

~39~

Matt

Tessa's fast. Warren sidles up behind me halfway through the mayor's semi-pastoral speech, telling me I better get her. I tell him to leave her alone, that she has a right to be angry. He starts cursing and by the time I realize it isn't aimed at me, Tessa's halfway to the mayor, surrounded by police but still shouting.

The rope in front of me disappears beneath a sea of feet as motorcycles roar to life, four of them peeling up the stairs to where police have formed a wall to protect the mayor. The air fills with a mixture of shrieks and shouts, some for the club and many against. Rocks begin to fly and police draw their weapons. In the middle of everything is my Tessa, hair flying in all directions as she shouts, "Thou shall not! Thou shall not!" working the parts of the crowd not already shouting into a frenzy.

Shoving Beth's hand off my arm, I head up the stairs. I need to get to Tessa before she gets shot. If one of these scared cops pulls a trigger, the club will open fire. I have no doubt they're armed.

Beth catches up to me, dragging me into her clutches once more. "Don't. The club will get her out."

I glare at her. "Or they'll get her killed."

Fury flashes across her face. "Chief loves her almost as much as that stupid biker gang does. No one is going to kill *her*. She's the only one safe out of all the women who are out here today!"

I push my keys into her hands. "Go. I'll get Tessa and meet you at the car."

"Matt…" she whispers.

I look up to where Tessa is climbing onto the back of Chopper's bike, finger in the air as she blows a kiss to Chief. My teeth grind against one another. Chopper's bike takes off down the stairs to the right of where I'm standing. Neither of them glance my way.

Biting down the anger, I cup Beth's elbow and pull her through the crowd, making our way to the car with the sound of bikes roaring all around us. Once the wolves got their girl, they pulled out. Soon it will just be the townspeople sitting around trying to figure out who they're mad at.

I open Beth's door, letting her slide into my shotgun seat. I take one last look around the plaza. Tessa and her club are gone. I drop into the driver's seat and slam the door. Every time I feel like I'm making progress with Tessa, having her trust me, need me, *want* me, she runs off. With Chopper. "Are you sure it's Warren your sister has kismet with? I'm starting to feel like there's a biker standing in the way of my happily ever after and it isn't Gary!"

~Tessa~

I'm blowing up Chief's phone and he's returning the favor, rubbing in how quickly he dispersed the crowd after the "troublemakers" left. What he really means is the only people who didn't leave are the ones controlled by fear. Those who will go along with a curfew as if it's actually going to do them any good. Samantha and Cheryl were both killed in the morning, but Chief refuses to relinquish the control he now has.

I throw my phone across the bar. Bear snatches it out of the air, proceeding to take selfies. I'm in no mood to be entertained. The guys might be jazzed from the display of force they put on today, but as far as I'm concerned, that showing didn't help anything. Gary is still in jail and now Chief gained back some of the power Gary took from him the night of our town hall meeting.

In my office, I study my cameras once more, hoping to find something I missed before. A shadow of a person I don't know, a glimpse of a shirt that doesn't belong to anyone allowed into the hallway that leads to my office and the stairwell to the apartments. Unfortunately, I rarely have my office door open and someone could slip through the back door, up the stairs, and into Gary's apartment without so much as rustling dust for me to see.

Knuckles rap against my door in short hard bursts. "Go away."

"It's me," Matt bites. "And Beth."

I push backward and run to the door, throwing it open and wrapping my arms around him. "Where have you been?"

He pries my arms off him and shoves them down in front of me, stare as hard as his knock had been. "I tried calling you but someone named *Bear* answered and told me I sounded pretty enough that he'd make *me* his girlfriend. I figured if he had your phone, you must be here. Or Chopper ditched your phone and took you off to who knows where again."

"It's not her fault, Matt. It's yours." Warren leans on the wall opposite us where I can see his smirking face over Matt's shoulder. "I warned him, Tessa. But little Matty didn't grab you so Chopper did, before you got all the little piggies riled up enough to lay hands on you. One wrong move and we'd be having a luau in town square right now."

Matt lets go of me, turning around to engage Warren, who knows exactly what he's doing. He's trying to get the Leidolf to kick Matt out of here themselves, and he's succeeding. They won't tolerate fighting they're not a part of, and normally I wouldn't care because they'd side with me, but Warren has weaseled his way into their protection so it will be Matt they turn on. And I'm confused as to why they even let Matt back here to begin with. They're toying with him somehow, and it's going to end badly for Matt.

Taking a slender metal letter opener off my desk, I cup the ebony handle in my fist and march into the hallway, ducking under Matt's arm and lifting my own, bringing the sharp point of the makeshift weapon down hard, aiming straight for Warren's neck. He jumps out of the way and Beth screams, diving into my office. Matt grabs me around the waist and walks backward, pulling me into the office with Beth and slamming the door.

Spinning me to face him, members of the club laughing in the hallway and taking bets on how long it will be before I kill Warren or Warren kills Matt, my boyfriend is no less angry than he was before. I don't blame him. Put his shoes on my feet and I'd feel the same. Disrespected.

I toss the letter opener onto the desk and reach a hand toward Beth, who's as far into the corner as she can get, chewing her lip raw. "Let's go home." I meet Matt's eyes. "The three of us. To *our* house."

Tension loosens in his jaw. "You're going to stay there with me?" I nod and his mouth relaxes, the corner almost ticking into a smile. "You're finally choosing me over them? Over *him*?"

I take his hands in mine, study them and then meet his gaze. "I have loyalty to the club. They have my back, like you saw today, and I have theirs. But you're the man I want to come home to every night, wake up with every morning, and spend all my days with." I grin as Beth lets out an "aw" followed by a little sniff. "Matt, when this is all over, I want to have a family with you."

<h1 style="text-align:center">~40~</h1>

Last night was strange. I pressed my luck and managed to walk out the front door of the Grille and get into Matt's car. No one stopped me, though two bikes followed us and the roar of engines shook the windows in my house every time the club rotated members throughout the night, which was much more often than usual.

Matt complained about their presence, the mood in the house somber even though we set up drinking games and played until even Beth was sloshed. And I never told Matt that even though he feels confident in his ability to protect me, I feel safer knowing the Leidolf are outside. All I did was kiss him between shots, putting his tongue to better use than complaining. At some point, that kissing got heavy enough that Beth peeled off and went to her room. What happened after that is a haze of images flashing through my aching head as I curl over the toilet, puking up what I'm sure is a kidney.

Matt darkens the doorway, looking as bad as I feel. "Here's some water."

I take the glass, spilling half on the floor. "Whatever we did last night, not even my fingers are working."

He squats in front of me, brushing the sticky hair from my face with a smile. "They worked just fine last night. *Very* fine."

"So I'm out of the doghouse?"

He laughs. "Not if you keep rewarding me every time I feel jealous."

He gets to his feet and turns the shower on. I close my eyes, tamping down the wave of nausea crashing over me. "It won't always be like this. After the murderer is locked up, everyone will stop losing their minds, including me."

"You're right, it won't be long before we fall into a normal routine." He comes back and kneels down. "Feel like taking a shower with me? I'm going to have to go take pictures of some houses I'm insuring and get the paperwork started. Then I'll come back and make you and Beth dinner."

I take his hands and let him pull me to standing, resting my weight against him. "Will you drop me at the bar on your way out?" He frowns and I tuck my head into his chest. "You can text me when you're finished working and I'll come back home with you." *If Chopper allows me to.*

"What about Beth?"

I shrug. "If she isn't working, she can come with me, or stay here and I'll have whoever is outside stay with her."

He sighs. "Before we got to the bar yesterday, she was already getting calls from people canceling their childcare so I doubt she's working, and you know she hates being around the club almost as much as I'm starting to. Can't you just stay here with her?"

I shake my head, immediately regretting the action. "I have work to do. Clients to account for. Chiefs to harass. Mayors to threaten."

"You're in no condition to be working today and I think you did enough damage to town hall yesterday, I'm surprised you and all the bikers *having your back* aren't in jail."

I slide down his body and take up residence on the floor, there will be no shower for me today. I'll be lucky to manage washing my face. "We'd have to do much worse for them to arrest us. Which reminds me that I have a curfew to break. No drinking tonight. Instead, I'm going to walk every street in this town."

He kneels down and lifts me into his arms. "I doubt your guard dogs are going to let you do that, and your boyfriend definitely isn't." He places me in the tub and removes my shirt. "But I will wash your hair for you. And I'll pick you up after work and bring you home, because this is where we should be at night, Tessa. In *our* house. Together."

~

It's already lunchtime when I hop off the back of Granger's bike and walk into the Grille. It isn't as busy as it normally is, probably because of yesterday's kerfuffle, but there are two people curled together in a booth enjoying their meal like lovers do, feeding each other bites in between laughing whispers. Rene's eyes go wide as I approach. Warren turns just in time to snatch his mug of beer off the table. I throw Rene's glass of water in his face and walk away.

The sanctuary room door is closed, explaining why the club's presence is sparse out front. I slip into my office, dropping with relief into my seat and pulling a packet of candied ginger from my desk drawer. Popping a piece into my mouth, quelling the upset in a stomach not made for whatever I dumped into it last night, I boot up my computer and try to focus on something other than the never-ending pain inside my skull.

Warren stomps into the room, shirtless, and slams a phone onto the desk in front of me. "There are better ways for you to get my clothes off so you take this call, sober up, and go apologize to Rene because without her, we wouldn't know half of what we do." He removes his palm from the phone. "Apologize to Marcie for what you did to her yesterday, too, because jealousy doesn't suit you any more than being a drunk does."

"I didn't see Marcie yesterday but if she wants to spread lies, I'll go see her today," I growl. "And the water here is free, so get your girlfriend another glass and pray her meddling in Gary's case doesn't get him convicted because if it does, I'm going to spill more than her drink."

He leaves the room, slamming the door behind him. I pick up the phone. "Hello?"

"I hear you've been raising Cain." Gary's voice rolls from the speaker. Tears slam into my eyes. I stifle the sob but he hears it. "Honey, this is why I haven't called you. It's hard for me to listen to you hurting, even harder to hear the kind of anger you just spit all over Warren. I'm not saying he doesn't deserve it, but I *am* saying you have to stop. That's not a request, Tessa, it's an order, and if I hear of you breaking my orders again, I'm going to rip through the walls of this jail and personally beat your tail."

~41~

If it were possible for Gary to break out of jail, I'd buck him at every turn. I'd wage war on the whole town, put myself in every dangerous situation I could find, and make sure it was all broadcast straight into his cell. But he won't be the one to come for me. He'll send Chopper. And it's clear to me that Chopper is trying to distance himself.

I pace my office, phone pressed to my ear to soak in every last drop of Gary's voice. "I need Chopper handling some transactions I already had set up before I got locked away; club business I don't trust anyone else to run point on, and things I don't want you anywhere near. And Chopper only trusts one other person with you right now. Warren."

I drop into my chair, head shaking. "Warren? I left town once, I won't do it again. With anyone. Not Chopper, and especially not *Warren.*"

Gary sighs. "If I tell you to vanish, it won't be a request. You'll go when I say and with who I say, and there won't be any coming back. I don't care if it's your sister's body they find in the street, you'll stay gone."

"Then it might as well be *my* body they find because I am *not* running away from home like a scared little girl! You, Chief, Warren and all the rest of the men in this town can shove your theories and your curfews because none of it has kept a single woman safe!"

"How do you know?" he barks. "You chatting with the murderer to know his plans? We're all doing the best we can, Tessa, and no one knows if the extra club presence has kept the murders at bay or not. But we're getting ready to find out, so instead of instigating riots and pitting Chief against us, make nice with the law and do your part."

"My part?" I snap. "All I ever do is *my* part!"

A growl snakes out of the phone. "Since I've been locked up, all I hear tell of is you defying Chopper, Montrose, and every other member so you can go run around with this new boy of yours who likes to help you circumvent the club."

"My actions have nothing to do with Matt."

He ignores my statement. "Chopper is leaving later today with a third of the men, Bear is leaving with another third, Montrose is staying behind to keep an eye on things. With so few numbers, I need you to stay inside the bar until Chopper returns. If you have to go out somewhere, Warren goes with you. No exceptions. No Matt. Warren has eyes on you day and night until Chopper gets back."

I sink my teeth into my cheek, battling tears. "Why are you punishing me? The other men aren't sending their wives and girlfriends away, and they don't have them under lock and key. If this is about Warren's stupid theory, he has as much in common with all these women as I do."

I can hear Gary scratching the hair of his beard. He does that when he's agitated. "You don't trust Warren, and for good reason. I *do* trust him, for good reason. Maybe not in everything, but outside of myself and Chopper, I agree with Chopper that there's no one else more trustworthy when it comes to watching out for you. So I'm not asking you to trust Warren, honey, I'm asking you to trust me."

"Matt," I whisper. "You can trust Matt."

"Chopper doesn't," he replies flatly. "You need to know the source before you go accusing Warren. He hasn't said much about the kid, but I'm aware of Warren's ulterior motives so even if he did, I wouldn't take it to heart. Chopper is another story. He saw something he didn't like the other night when he had to break up the fight in my apartment. He called me when you snuck out to go to the kid's place and I told Chopper to let it be, so he did, but I'm torn between trusting you to be the smart girl I always knew you to be and believing Chopper isn't speaking from jealousy when he tells me the boy doesn't fit."

I stare at the wall, the spot where I have a hidden camera. How many secrets am I willing to keep from Gary? "Did it ever occur to you that what I like about Matt is that he doesn't fit? He isn't rowdy, he's calm. Until Warren aggravates us. But Matt is my balance in this life. With him, I'm…"

"Drunk," Gary whispers. "That bit I did hear from Warren. He says you've been drinking a lot and that you look like a semi ran over you. Whether or not that's Matt's fault the way Warren says, or if it's because you're crumbling over what's happening, I need you to promise me you'll lay off the booze."

"That's rich coming from a bar owner."

He laughs, genuinely this time. I spin my chair into the desk and rest my head on the cool wood. "Matt isn't forcing me to drink, it's the other way around, because I *am* crumbling. The one person I love the most in this world was arrested, charged with murdering multiple women, and he won't talk to me, but he talks to everyone else."

"You can dump a beer over my head when I get out." The smile in his voice is short-lived. "I need you to bury Samantha for me, Tess."

I sit up. "You'll be out soon. We'll do it together."

"I'm not getting out for a long while, you and I both know it." He speaks softly. "Take money out of the safe and check on Sam's mom again. She's too proud to call and ask for help so just take her groceries and pay some bills for her. Then, you two set the date and lay my girl to rest."

My eyes flood as his voice cracks. "I'll take care of it. Sam will have the ceremony you were planning."

"Thank you," he whispers. "When I get out, I'll pay my respects and sit with her grave a while."

I mop the tears from my cheeks. "I love you, Gary."

"I love you too, honey. That's why I need you to stop bucking me. I can't lose you. So make up with Chief and play nice with Warren because you're not Montrose's favorite person and I don't trust him as far as I can throw him. The men handling the bar are loyal to me, but you keep Warren beside you and if he tells you to run, you go and don't look back."

~

My heart slows in my chest as I climb the stairs to Gary's apartment. I'm going to have to tell Matt I'm not coming home. Again. Opening the door, I freeze. Warren is on the couch running a knife over a smooth stone. He puts the stone on the table and sheaths the sleek metal, eyebrow lifting. "Gary put you in your place or do I need to buy a dozen new shirts?"

"Why do you have that knife?"

He chuckles. "You live in a bar full of men with guns and it's my knife that worries you?"

I toss him his phone. "A toothpick in your hands worries me, and that knife sure looks like it could do the damage that's been done to the dead women."

He takes the knife back out of the sheath. "This curve right here on the tip," he taps it, "it's called a gut hook. This here," he points to a saw-like feature at the base of the blade, "yeah, Tessa, this is the kind of knife that can do some damage. And I keep it sharp just for that reason."

"Is that a threat? Because Chopper hasn't left yet and I'm sure he'd love to hear all about your knife."

He gets off the couch, undoing the buckle on his belt as he stalks toward me. "That smart girl I used to know really is gone, isn't she? You're all boozed up now and weak between the ears. No wonder you're with a pansy insurance salesman."

I watch his hands feed his belt through the loop of the sheath, fixing the knife into place on his hip. His hands are different than Matt's. Where Warren is slender and long, Matt is beefy and wide. Where Warren is calloused and scarred, Matt is smooth and tender. I lift my gaze. "Drunk, hungover, or even dumber than a rock, I still know Matt's a better man on his worst day than you *ever* were on your best."

His eyes spark. "Chopper left five minutes after you got on the phone with Gary, and since he left me in charge of you, I'd say I'm head and shoulders above every other man in your life. Tell that to your boyfriend when he calls. And don't leave out the part where I'll be right here, with my eyes *all* over you."

<h1 style="text-align:center">~42~</h1>

I thought I was done with puking for the day but Warren brought out the best of what my stomach had to offer. Unlike Matt, Warren didn't bring me water or even attempt to wipe my face. When I emerged from the bathroom he was kicked back on the couch, scrolling through his phone with the television tuned to a basketball game.

Scouring the cabinets for crackers, I pull a box of saltines from the pantry and dial Beth. "Hey." I keep her on speaker. "Can you bring me my car? I'll drop you back off at home later."

"Sure. Where'd you leave it parked?"

"Um, I don't really remember. I was hoping you'd seen it?"

"Nope." She sighs. "I only know where *my* car is because I don't have a revolving door of men to chauffeur me around everywhere."

"Wonder why?" Warren mutters behind me.

I shoot him a glare, glad she didn't hear him. "You have Arnold. Why don't you go stay with him tonight?"

She laughs. "And miss you and Matt going at each other like rabbits? You two are *sooo* loud."

I lean on the counter. "Sorry about that. Last night was…a much-needed release of tension."

She adds a purr into her laugh this time. "It sure sounded like you got *released*. Several times."

Her words get Warren unglued from the couch. He's up and slamming the door behind him before I get a chance to flip him off. "Look, I won't be coming back home tonight so it would be really helpful if you'd go to Arnold's."

"Why?" she whines. "What about Matt? Is he going to be here?"

I lean my head back, feeling sick again. "I don't know, Beth. Right now I'm focused on Samantha's funeral. Her body is being released and Gary wants to go ahead with the service right away. Have you heard what the plans for Cheryl are?"

"Day after tomorrow." She huffs. "I told you that already."

I rub my temples. "It must have slipped my mind. We'll do Samantha's two days after Cheryl. That gives the club time to get back in town."

"They're gone?"

I bite my lip, I shouldn't have said anything about the club's movements. "Some of them took off on a ride this morning, ones that will want to be here to pay respects to Samantha. Especially with Gary being locked up."

"Sounds like code for them being up to no good. Do you think they went off to kill someone?" She gasps. "Like on a hit?"

"No," I fire back. "And this isn't the time to joke about things like that."

"Who's joking?"

"Go to Arnold's," I order. "And if you find out where I left my car, let me know."

I head downstairs with no intention of telling Warren where I'm going. In my office, I slide the tallest filing cabinet out of its place and over to the front of the cabinet beside it. Stooping to the face of the safe, I input the code and open the door. The stacks of cash are exactly as I left them, minus the amounts that go into the daily deposits. Only a handful of people have the combination to this safe, and even fewer have the combination for the safe hidden behind this one. I stare at the spot where a shelf pops out to reveal another keypad—one that opens a door to the hidden room. I don't have the code for it but Gary has always said I'd figure it out if I ever needed to. And I'd only need to if he was dead.

I don't doubt that Chopper was in the secret safe at some point before he left. I only hope he comes back in one piece. The Leidolf usually do, being that they're more militaristic than outlaw, but they all have scars and I've witnessed more than a few injuries being patched up. I close my eyes and hope Chopper can feel my heart. "Be safe."

I wipe the tears that come from the heartache of him not even bothering to say goodbye to me, then take two stacks of twenties that are bundled into groups of five hundred and two stacks of hundreds that are bundled into groups of twenty-five hundred. This should cover Samantha's mom and get a down payment started on the funeral. I'll grab the rest of what I need later.

Even though I'm sure my car isn't here, I slip out the back door and check the lot, glad to see that Rick and Randy are still here. "Either of you seen my wheels lately?" They shake their heads and I go back inside to check with the bar staff, only to get the same answer. No one has seen my vehicle.

Bypassing the stool Warren's sitting on, I go to Freddie. "I need a ride."

He grins. "I knew you'd coming begging one day."

I roll my eyes. "Not that kind of ride."

He chuckles. "You know I'd take you, but I have orders. Big man over there with his crocodile knife has you until Chops gets back."

"Doesn't it bother you that a random person shows up in our bar mysteriously wielding the power to have his way? And that he also has a woman-gutting knife on him?"

Warren gets off his stool, fingers circling my wrist. "You might be trying to get your boyfriend killed but I'm not him anymore, sweetheart. You want to leave this bar, you leave with me. You don't want my ride? Sit anywhere you like and make yourself at home."

He lets go of me, waiting. I march out the front door. He follows me. "You develop a death wish to go along with your drinking habit?" I keep walking, ignoring him. "Tessa!" He shouts my name. I move faster. His sun-weathered arm snakes around my waist, jerking me to a stop. "I don't want to be here babysitting you any more than you want me here. I'd rather be at work, making sure my business isn't being run into the ground, but with dead women falling from the sky, we've all lost our right to do what we want." He lets me go. "You can keep throwing tantrums and fighting me, or you can choose to let me do what I'm supposed to do because you don't know *half* of the kind of danger you're in."

I move my mouth slowly, so he can hear me annunciate each word. "No. One. Is. Trying. To. Kill. Me."

His head shakes. "You think killing you is the only bad thing a man can do?"

"No, but it's the worst."

The smug exterior he's wearing falls away and his eyes stare in a way that sends shivers through me. His voice is barely audible. "They can do things that would make you wish you were dead. And all of them will be worse, Tessa."

I look away, focusing on the bar's front parking lot. "I'm aware that Montrose doesn't like me but he would never make a move against me."

Warren steps close to me and wraps his fingers around my waist when I try to move away. "There's a power struggle going on. Montrose wants Gary out so he can lead the club into business ventures that keep getting defeated in a vote count because of Gary and those loyal to him. Montrose will *absolutely* drag Gary's pride and joy into the center of his war, and if the leverage doesn't make Gary cave, what Montrose does to you next *will.*"

I falter, hands gripping Warren's forearms before I realize I'm holding onto him. I remove my touch and take a steadying breath. "Money motivates people to do stupid things, which makes me wonder how much you think this club war is going to profit you. That's how you gained entry into the deepest parts of Gary's life, isn't it? Me? His greatest weakness used against him." His fingers loosen and I take a step backward. "What did you do, Warren? Tell him only your love can save me?" I say the words mockingly and anger flashes through his irises.

He grips my elbow and drags me back toward the bar. "We're not kids stealing pudding cups from the cafeteria anymore, Tessa. This is the big leagues, and two of the biggest dogs in the league are nervous." He pulls me around to the back parking lot, grip not easing when Rick and Randy see us. Gary really did give Warren authority where I'm concerned.

He shoves me toward a Harley Low Rider, plucking a helmet from the back and handing it to me. My nostrils flare. "You *are* trying to join the club."

He straddles the bike, pushing a helmet over his own head and lifting the visor, mouth drawing tight. "I've got your car. You're not getting it back. Now shut your mouth and get on my bike."

~43~

Warren tries to make me lose my grip on his bike. He gooses the engine, trying to bounce me forward or off. I'm not quite sure if he wants to make me hold onto him or get a concussion. Either way, I know how to squeeze my thighs and balance my body. And the only reason I got onto his bike to begin with is because I have business to take care of.

He goes ahead of me into Norma Kay's trailer, offering his condolences and walking through the home before taking up a silent vigil near a front window while I ask Norma Kay about her needs. From the looks of her home, she's become a hoarder since the last time I visited.

I clean up her kitchen and then call the bar, asking for someone to be sent to finish scrubbing the house. After that, I say my goodbyes and slide into place behind Warren. He starts his bike and we drive out of the trailer park, my hands gripping the bike itself. But my stance on not touching him won't quell the rumors. If Warren had stayed with his bike and kept his helmet on, no one would have known it was him. But he had his mop of dark hair out in view of all the neighbors, and they were all looking, so now they'll be speculating as to whether or not the old flames are back together. I only hope the rumor doesn't reach Matt. Not before I have a chance to explain why I'm out with Warren.

At least Warren drives to the funeral home like he actually knows how to handle a bike. Inside the building, he takes a back seat again, not saying anything other than hello to the staff. He's only here to shadow me, but normally I'm not so aware of my shadow.

Nancy is fairly new to town, the granddaughter of the man who used to run this funeral home. After he died, she took over. "I'll give you a few minutes alone." She speaks softly, leaving me to peruse the caskets. I walk slowly through the rows, chest tight with grief. One day someone will have to do this for me, choose my eternal resting box, and if there's truth to any of Warren's words, that might happen sooner than I'd like.

Stopping at an antique-white casket with a pale rose inlay, I run my hand over the butterflies carved along the edge. Warren comes up beside me, staring down into the folds of satin fabric. "Sam would like this."

Tears rim my eyes. "You think so?"

He nods. "Do you remember that time we were up on the cliffs above the river? When Sam showed up buzzed and leaned over the edge trying to take pictures of caterpillars?"

I laugh, sending tears cascading over my cheeks. "There were gobs of them in the trees growing just beneath the ledge. I'd never seen anything like it."

He smiles. "She kept saying we were all caterpillars, and that one day we'd get our wings."

Warren saved Samantha that day. He held her tight, let her get her pictures and then pulled her from the edge and stood between her and it as she spun and danced in that late summer sun. School was about to start back for us, my and Warren's senior year. We spent that night talking about all the flying we would do with those wings once we graduated.

I rest my hand on the butterflies. "Go tell them we choose this one. It's perfect for Samantha."

~

Today's been emotional. I'm drained from crying, from fighting, from not being able to see Matt in person. I just want to eat the bowl of macaroni I microwaved and go to bed. "Matt,

I don't blame you for being upset that I'm not coming home again." I set the hot macaroni bowl on a dish towel, burning my fingers in the process as I balance the phone between my shoulder and ear. "I swear I'll make all of this up to you. I already have some ideas about how to celebrate your birthday next week."

"All I want is for you to be in this relationship *with* me."

"I am." I lean my forehead against the cabinet above the counter where my macaroni is cooling. "I'm being pulled in every direction, Matt. I'm exhausted, confused, and every second I'm not with you, I feel utterly alone."

He blows out a breath. "I know, babe. I feel the same way. Which is why I want you to come home. I've spent more nights in your house without you than I have *with* you."

I lift away from the cabinet. "Just keep our bed warm and I'll be back in it with you soon. And send me pictures of the waffles you're eating without me, and maybe a few shots of you topless."

He chuckles. "You've got it. I might even rub myself in butter for you."

Tears run down my face. I haven't told him I was with Warren today or that Warren is five feet from me right now. Matt wouldn't be so loving and understanding if he knew. "Now that you've given me sweet dreams, I'll let you go. I love you, Matt."

"I love you, too. I'll talk to you in the morning."

Hanging up, I palm the dish towel that's under my single-serve bowl and walk past the couch. Warren speaks for the first time since we left the funeral home. "You can't keep dating him. The sooner you break things off, the better. For both of you."

"Thank you for your concern, but it's none of your business."

Slamming Gary's bedroom door shut, I crawl onto the bed and stab a fork through the macaroni. Warren knocks on the door, opening it without waiting for an invitation. He puts his hands up in truce. "I only want to tell you something."

"I've heard everything I need to hear from you."

He lowers his hands and leans a shoulder against the doorframe. "I got the city contract because I found out Mayor Smith was shooting porn in the stockroom of the Christian bookstore he owns over in Fayetteville."

I drop the bowl, unfeeling to the hot macaroni on my legs. "He what?"

Warren picks up the overturned bowl and starts scraping the macaroni back inside. "It's pretty hard-core stuff. He wears a devil mask and drills this hairdresser chick, yelling about being the son of Satan and asking her how he *feels*."

I'm as pale as the macaroni, preferring to eat mine without cheese. Warren's jaw works. "When the good church elder-turned-mayor started spouting that Bible crap the other day, I wanted to do what you did. But I've already played my leverage. I can't touch him."

I realize his hands are all over my legs and move away. "What about his family? His poor wife!"

Warren straightens. "She knows. That's how I found out. She blamed the hairdresser, saying the girl corrupted her husband and well, there's nothing quite like a scorned hairdresser. The chick came to a party I was at and pulled up the website they sold the videos to, telling everyone she was getting ready to get paid because of the *high-profile* man under the mask. A few drinks in, I pried a name out of her. Then I talked to a couple of her coworkers and showed them a picture of Mayor's wife—they confirmed she was the woman who came into their salon calling their fellow hairdresser a Jezebel."

"And then you blackmailed the mayor?"

He shrugs. "Everything he and that girl did was consensual, even what looked to me like it would be painful for her. She said she liked it. So all Mayor had to do was be honest with the public about who he is. He chose to hide behind his *faith* and give me a contract to keep my mouth shut. That's on him."

"Do I know this girl?"

His head shakes. "Doubtful. She's from Fayetteville, too. The salon she works for is in the same mall as Mayor's bookstore, that's how they met. I guess he thought doing the deeds in a different county wouldn't leak back to him here, but I like to get around because a man learns a lot from just sitting in corners and listening."

"Yeah, well, you're not sitting in my corner. See yourself out. Preferably into oncoming traffic."

He rolls his eyes, heading back to the door nonetheless. "Give it a rest, Tessa. You're boring." He spins around to look at me as he closes the door. "You're also sloppy. The pig's influence. Dump him."

~44~

Despite the chill that surrounds us, Warren and I are managing to argue less. He even made himself scarce when Beth came to drop off clothes for both Cheryl's service and Samantha's. I didn't have to ask him to either. All I had to do was mention she'd be dropping by and I didn't see him again until well after she was gone. That allowed me to not have to answer her questions or worry about her blabbing to Matt that I've been rooming with my ex.

For Cheryl's funeral, Warren let Matt pick me up, following us on his bike and waiting in the flanks. I never saw him, but I knew he was there from the way the tiny hairs on the back of my neck would stand on end. I imagine that's when his eyes were on me instead of the crowd. It used to be that way in school anyway. I'd be across a room or sitting on the opposite end of the cafeteria and my skin would prick. I'd look up and there would be Warren, watching me.

Today we're at Samantha's repast, and things with Warren aren't the same as they were at Cheryl's funeral. Warren is welcome among the crowd. And Chopper is back, keeping himself positioned close to me. He was delayed getting home and didn't show up until just before Samantha's funeral started, so I haven't broached the subject of returning to my own house yet. And now that the funeral is over and we're all gathered in the bar to have food and tell stories of Sam, the time doesn't feel right.

It doesn't feel right to exclude Matt, either. He's with me, arm curled around me on our side of the booth as Beth sits opposite us. His lips press against my temple, mouth lowering to my ear. "It's probably inappropriate to say this, but you look beautiful."

I rest my head against his chest and close my eyes. I've missed this. Him. The steady thrum of his heart. "You're highly inappropriate, but I like it."

Beth brings up the topic I'm trying to avoid. "Are you coming home with us?"

I feel Matt's body tense. I open my eyes and look at Beth. "I have to discuss it with Chopper."

Matt groans but doesn't say anything. Beth plops her chin in her hands. "You better do it soon or we're going to miss curfew."

"Screw the curfew."

She sticks out her tongue. "Says the one person who won't get arrested for breaking it."

"No one is going to get arrested for breaking curfew, Chief is just trying to scare people."

Matt's fingers graze along my shoulder. "I thought you two made up? You were friendly at the service earlier."

I shrug. "Gary told me I had to be, so I apologized a couple of days ago and sent three dozen donuts to the station this morning."

He chuckles. "That's my diplomatic woman."

Beth smiles. "Like I said, *you* can break the law and not get in trouble. I can't. So let's just leave. Why do you have to stay here anyway? I mean, I was against the curfew but there haven't been any murders since it went into effect, right?"

"I highly doubt that's because the psycho is scared of a curfew."

She leans forward, whispering. "I heard that there were footprints in the mud by the road where Isabel's body was found. And do you remember that one serial killer in California? The one they *caught* because he left footprints everywhere?" I shake my head and her eyes go wide. "They tracked down the type of shoe and even the *color* of it, just by the tread of the print that was left." She sits up. "They can find out *anything* about *anyone* these days."

"Except who's murdering people in our town," I scoff, looking up at Matt. "Is that true? Footprints were found near Isabel's body?"

He glances at Beth and then back at me. "I haven't heard that, but Beth talks to more people around here than I do."

She remains silent, letting us decide for ourselves if we believe her or not. I rub my eyes. "All I know is no one has been arrested other than Gary, and not even the club has dug up anything helpful."

"How are they compiling their leads?" Matt asks. "Are they even getting any?"

I think of Warren saying he learns a lot just by sitting around listening and my eyes snap to Chopper. He's at a table a few feet away from us, head down as usual, staring into a mug of beer. I search for Warren and find him at the end of the bar where Chopper normally sits. His head isn't down but he isn't engaging with the people around him either. He's listening. "Peas in a pod."

"What?" Matt's fingers slip over my jaw and turn me to face him, a smile drawing his lips high and wide. "That's better. Now I can see your beautiful face."

Beth's nails tap over the table. "I heard the club has been roughing people up to *make* them talk. They're riding the streets at night, interrogating every man they see."

"So?" I shrug. "I'd rather them harass people than have bodies dropping all around us."

Matt pulls me onto his lap, hand resting over the knee that's exposed beneath my black pencil skirt. I thought the black and white print blouse with the flouncy tie at the neck was too much on its own and completely over the top when paired with the sleek skirt and red heels, but Beth insisted, and both the funeral outfits she brought were similar. Nothing else in my closet at home or at Gary's was appropriate so I had no choice but to go with Beth's picks.

"So," Matt begins, "whether the club is getting information the wrong or right way, I think I can help them put it all in one place." His fingers tighten as his eyes meet mine. "I have a vested interest in moving this whole murder thing along."

"Oh yeah?" I grin. "What exactly can you do?"

"I'll compile the information I'm given, feed the details into a spreadsheet built to link all the data together for us. It will find any connections we might have otherwise missed."

"What kind of connections?" Beth asks.

He looks down at my shoes. I nearly wore my boots but one of the girls at the bar saw the heels and said Samantha would appreciate them. Matt's fingers intentionally tickle my foot as he slips one of the shoes off. "Say they *did* find shoe prints at one of the scenes but the information hasn't been made public yet. In the meantime, one of the Leidolf notes talking to a man wearing red shoes. A different member mentions talking to a man with muddy red shoes in his trunk. The program will link those bits of data so if the police ever say their suspect has red shoes, well, we've got a ready-made lead for them." He slips the shoe back onto my foot with a wink. "It'll be a lot of work, and the club will have to either write down absolutely everything they've seen and heard, or they'll have to come to my office and let me record them so I can pull the bits of data out later."

My gut pinches, mouth going dry. He sounds like a cop. A cop finding a clever way to get information from the club. "Can you build the program and teach me to use it?"

He nods. "I was hoping you'd be my sidekick. And if we do it right, we might even open our own detective agency. Give you something to do other than instigate riots."

~45~

Chopper allowed me to go home with Matt and Beth. He followed, along with Warren. Beth asked me who was on the second bike, and I said I didn't know in order to avoid the conflict of confessing that it was Warren under that helmet. Most of the guys don't wear helmets with visors. Most of them don't wear helmets at all. I'm glad Warren is choosing to cover every speck of his mug. I'm also glad that Beth doesn't know Warren's body as well as I do. He'd have to do a lot more than cover his face to hide who he is from me.

When Chopper parked behind us, Warren kept going. When I got inside the house, I went to my bedroom to change, peeking out the window that overlooks the backyard to see if Warren had parked on the street that the house behind mine fronts, slipping through their shrubbery in the darkness, giving himself a view of my house. A view of the window I'm in now, the one that belongs to the bedroom I'd meant to share with him.

"What are you looking at?" Matt whispers, coming up behind me and sliding his big arms around my waist.

"Nothing." I let the curtain fall and spin in his arms. "It's nice to be home."

He presses his forehead to mine. "Since the club wants you under house arrest, I thought I'd buy a little kiddie pool and build you a beach out there." I laugh and he kisses my neck. "I even found some inflatable palm trees on the internet."

I drape my arms around his neck. "Inflatable palm trees are only one of the *many* reasons I love you."

He smiles. "Then can I draw you a bath? And sit in it with you?"

My heart thunders. "This vacation is sounding better by the minute."

~

I wake to the sound of Beth screaming. The bedroom door is open and Matt is running down the hall. I stumble out of bed, pulling sheets around me and trying to remember where exactly I am. "Matt!" I yell, mouth feeling like rot.

He steps into the hall, his boxers askew and his hair sticking up. But it's the set of his jaw and the purplish tinge to his neck that has my attention. "Did you tell Warren he could come here?"

"No way." Beth backs out of the kitchen, round eyes focused on what I can only assume is Warren. "She wouldn't let you in this house."

I press my back against the wall and slide onto the floor. "How much did I drink last night?"

Warren steps into the hall in front of Beth, sipping from a pink pig-nose cup that Mom bought me as a housewarming gift because she thought it would make a "nice start to a country theme".

"Jeez, Tessa." Warren frowns. "Didn't we talk about your drinking?"

"Why are you talking to her about anything?" Matt yells.

Warren makes a show of taking another sip from his pig cup. "One of us has to be responsible for her."

"Get off your high horse," Matt snaps. "She deserved a drink after yesterday, and a whole bottle after what she's been made to go through." He points at the floor. "*This* is her home." His finger presses into his chest. "*I'm* her home."

Warren tips his cup at me. "Thanks for the coffee. We're leaving in fifteen. I'll be out front."

"Where's Chopper?" I ask.

He walks to the front door, leaving his cup on the card table, answering me with one word. One single word that makes all the difference. "Gone."

That means I can't stay here. I have to get dressed and go with him.

I reach for Matt. "Help me up."

Beth hurries toward me, her nightshirt unbuttoned one button too far and mascara smeared under her eyes. "What is *he* doing here?"

Matt doesn't touch me so I push myself sideways and crawl back into my room. "Gary's orders. Yell at him if you don't like it."

Matt follows me into the room, putting away all the clothes I manage to yank from the hangers in my closet. "I don't have a choice, Matt." I crawl past him and into the bathroom. He follows, turning the bathtub water off directly after I turn it on. "Can I at least brush my teeth?"

His teeth grind. "You can tell your ex to get off your property."

"I never told him he could be here to begin with. Gary did. So take your grievances up with the boss because if you haven't been paying attention, *I* don't get to have a say in what happens in *my* life!"

My voice rises with each word, Matt's following suit. The shouting brings Warren back in the door. He shoulders past Matt and stares at me crumpled in a pile of sheets on the bathroom floor. He reaches past me and turns on the tub, looking back at Matt. "Spike the coffee I left on the table and bring the water pitcher from the refrigerator." He focuses back on me, hand resting on my forehead. "The caffeine will help, but you're going to have to drink a lot of water in between sips. Okay?"

"I don't want to go to the bar today."

He nods, eyes hardening. "I'll call Chops, but he's going to be pissed. If he'd known you were in this kind of shape…Tess, this isn't you."

Matt slams a glass of water onto the sink. "Get out. *I* can take care of *my* girlfriend."

Warren straightens, stepping into Matt, the two men chest to chest. "I'm going to go make a call and when I get back, she better be off of this floor."

~

The next time I wake up, I'm back in my own bed. Warren is leaning against the doorframe. "Where's Matt?"

"Out."

I sit up, head pounding. "What did you do to him?"

"He's with Beth. After you fell asleep they went on some kind of store run." He takes a step inside the room. "How are you feeling?"

"Better."

"Liar." He grins, looking around the room. "Nice place—"

"Yeah, and it could have been yours but you're a loser, and I'm tired of talking to you."

His jaw ticks. "I was saying that you have a nice place, but you're not as secure here as you are at the bar."

I wave my hands in the air, mocking fright. "Aside from the murderer, isn't it club members you're worried about?"

He nods. "A handful of them. We're sure the rest have your back but *if* we calculated wrong, it's a mistake none of us will be able to live with. So if you stay here and one of them knocks on your door, which are you going to let in?"

"Give me names of who you don't trust and I'll make sure they don't get my engraved invitation."

"No can do." He takes out his phone, fingers moving over the buttons. "Chopper is busy—and irate, by the way—so if you stay here, I have to stay with you. Which means I'll be inside because I've been outside all night. I'm tired, hungry, and I also need a shower and a change of clothes."

I glance at the closet and swing my legs over the side of the bed. "Matt can lend you some clothes when he gets back. Until then, you're welcome to what's in the kitchen and you can nap in here. I'm getting up."

"Like I want to sleep in the bed you share with *him*."

"Then take Beth's!" I scream. "That's where you always wanted to be anyway."

~46~

Lying on the lounger, soaking up the sun with my head in Matt's lap and my toes in the sand he spread around the four-foot-wide kiddie pool, I pretend Warren isn't here. That he didn't get into my shower when Matt finally returned home. I haven't spoken to Warren since I yelled at him, and all he said to Matt was, "You're up, pig."

Matt is irritated and I've told him I'm no less aggravated. I don't understand a situation that gets *Warren* being a third to Gary. If Montrose wants to *capture* me for leverage, then being at the bar is only safe if Montrose doesn't have enough support to overthrow Gary. Chopper and Gary wanting me locked up there leads me to believe Montrose is barking up a losing tree. Which means *he* isn't why they're spooked. *He* isn't who they think is murdering women to get at Gary. What they think is that someone else is out there. Someone more menacing than Montrose could ever hope to be. And they're *certain* I'm a target, if not *the* target. And all the other murders are meant to…torture me? Torture Gary?

"Are you going to be sick again?" Beth asks from her own lounger.

"No." I stretch my hand across to her. She helped Matt set this whole beach thing up. They even attached a sprinkler to the water hose so a delicate mist falls over us as we bake in the sun. She locks her fingers through mine, and Matt rubs my shoulders, working the tension out. "I'm feeling much better."

I focus on Matt's touch and attempt to block the dark thoughts that are never far from me anymore. Doing so brings visions of Warren dancing through my head, an odd mix of emotions stirring in my gut. I despise him, that emotion sings loud and clear among all the others. But another equally vocal feeling is loss. My whole world broke when things ended between us, and I can't ever get the years I gave him back. I can't ever get rid of the resentment he implanted into me for Beth. She didn't do anything wrong with him, nothing I fault her for anyway. But I still harbor ill feelings toward her. And I'm doing it while knowing that if I'm a target of this murderer, then so is she. Another bad thing that will happen to her because of me.

"Well, isn't this a darling little beach setup." Warren blots out my sun, stealing my breath when my eyes drop to the gray sweatpants hanging on his hips. He sees my gaze and smiles. "I always wondered what happened to these. Thanks for keeping my clothes all these years, *babe*."

Matt sits up. "I swear to God I'm going to kill him."

I press myself against him so he has to lie back down. "Just ignore him."

Warren tugs up the bottom of his pants and steps into the kiddie pool. "What are we celebrating?"

None of us answer. Beth is a statue. I don't even think she's breathing. Warren stretches. "Zeno is coming to watch the house, so no one try to go anywhere while I catch a few hours of sleep. And Beth, I'm not drunk, and I'm a light sleeper, so stay out of my room."

Matt's chest thunders. "You don't have a room here! You're a guard dog, so go sleep on the porch."

Warren strolls away with a laugh. He baits Matt and Matt bites every single time. The back door slides shut just as the roar of Zeno's bike rolls over the house. I drop my head back onto Matt's chest and close my eyes. "It won't always be like this. Let's just keep reminding ourselves of that."

His hands rest on my hips. "You kept his clothes? Those oversized shirts in your closet, they're all his?"

Beth sucks in a breath and blows it out. "Tessa wore that stuff more than he did and bought half of it, *that's* why she kept it."

Matt huffs. "He still rummaged through her closet, though. Did Gary give him permission to do that, too?"

"Can we just pretend he isn't here?" I groan. "And celebrate the fact that I *am* here?"

He takes a calming breath. "Depends. Are you allowed to have a drink in celebration, or is that now forbidden, too?"

~

With a cooler full of beer, compliments of Beth, we turned up the music and I forgot about the rest of the world until I went into the house to grab towels. Tiptoeing into the back of the house, I peek into my room. Warren isn't in the bed. My heart constricts, the pain of him choosing Beth's bed over mine opening up the old wound as if the knife is freshly planted in my flesh. While I've been outside for the last three hours, he's been spreading himself all over my sister's sheets. I shouldn't care, but I do.

My closet door is ajar. I move into the room to shut it, hoping he's finished rummaging through my things. I trip over his booted feet. He's on the floor, his back against the wall, head resting on his left arm while his right hand rests atop a pistol. Not the one from my nightstand, a newer model, like the one Chopper carries. "This looks safe." I stoop down, sliding the metal from under his fingers. I do recall him being a light sleeper but he's out cold, his mouth slightly open, his chest rising and falling softly.

Opening the chest at the end of my bed, I take out one of the blankets Arlene crocheted for me. I bought the cedar chest just to preserve these in because they're the nicest things anyone has ever given me. She was a cook in my high school and I'd talk to her sometimes, mostly so Warren could steal snacks from the pantry, but I truly liked her stories. As a graduation gift, she made me these two blankets. Her hands were already tight with arthritis by then so her making these for me is all the more meaningful.

I pull the lightest of the two over Warren's exhausted frame. It's hot outside, but the air conditioner is doing its job inside. And everyone sleeps better when there's something warm covering them.

I move back to the door. "Tessa." He whispers my name.

I turn around, his eyes are still closed. Only his mouth moves. "The ceremony was nice. I didn't get to tell you that yesterday, but you sent Samantha off right. She's flying now."

~47~

It's nights like these that make me think of Warren. Backyard barbecues, loud music, and the dark corners where lovers can hide away and get lost in a fevered kiss. Only, Warren is across the lawn from me and Matt is manning the grill, handling the unannounced arrival of eighteen Leidolf like a boss. I'm still sitting in my lounger, having moved it close enough to the pool to rest my feet in the cool liquid. In years gone by, a night like this would end with a dip in the river.

Tonight, though, my feet are all that are going to get wet. I'm not even drinking. Not after the near catastrophe that happened when Chopper showed up. He was heading for Matt. Warren stopped him, the two of them tussling until Warren said something that made Chopper stop. I didn't hear what was said and Matt had no idea that he was about to lose his head because he'd been too busy grumbling about all the unexpected bikers crashing our party. All Matt saw was Chopper's hand snaking around my arm. Chopper took me into the house and set down a new law. No more drinking.

I didn't have to tell Matt what was said, he guessed, and has smartly kept his opinions about it to himself. So has Beth, because she took the first burger Matt cooked and disappeared into her bedroom. I haven't seen her since. All I'm doing is sitting in my little spot watching Matt. He has a beer in his fist and is joking around with Dillon, Bear, and Freddie. Chopper is beside me. Silent. Angry.

"Are you staying here tonight?" I whisper.

"Warren is."

"I'd rather it be you."

"Tough."

"Anyone else, or just him?"

Chopper doesn't answer me. I get out of my chair. "I'm going to bed. Is that okay with you or is there a new rule about my bedtime?"

"I'll be here to get you in the morning. Be ready. If I have to wait, I'm going to crack his skull."

"Matt's birthday is tomorrow. I want to take him to dinner someplace nice. Out of town. Away from all of this. And maybe stay in a fancy hotel."

Chopper's eyes meet mine. "There is no place *away* from this. You can go to dinner, then you come back here." I open my mouth and he shakes his head. If I push, he'll take my dinner privilege away.

I lean toward him. "Do me a favor. Find the killer. And then get back to being the man I *still* want to believe you are."

~

I won't give Chopper credit for the fact that I feel better this morning than I've felt in a long while. Matt is beside me, hand tucked behind his head. "Good morning, handsome."

His jaw ticks. "Warren stayed in the house last night."

My heart thuds. "On the couch?"

He shrugs. "Beth got up to use the bathroom and found him in living room. She came and got me, and I told him he could stay outside. But he said he'd take *me* outside. As in fight me."

Matt isn't banged up so they didn't fight. That's good. "Sounds like I slept through a fun time."

He shifts. "Your sister went to her room and was scared to come back out."

"It was the middle of the night, she didn't need to be out."

"You're taking up for him?"

I get out of bed, so unbelievably tired of arguing with everyone. "Warren isn't going to hurt Beth and she knows it, so if she's in her room peeing in cups, that's her own problem. As for him being in the living room, that's something you have to take up with Gary. Like I've *already* told you ten thousand times." I shove my hands through my hair. "I'm not having the same conversation over and over. If you can't deal with the club's rules, you're free to leave."

He sits up. "Is that what you want?"

I shake my head. "No, Matt. I want you here. I want to ignore everything that we can possibly ignore and find a way to steal tiny moments of happiness because when I first opened my eyes, I *did* feel happy. Then you opened your mouth, and not to tell me anything good." I sit on the bed and run a hand over his leg. "It's your birthday. I want you to have as much joy as we can suck out of this day." I lean over and kiss his thigh. "I'm taking you to dinner tonight, but you can have dessert now."

~

Beth starts in on me the instant I emerge from my bedroom. I brush her off. "You're out of your room now, Beth. That's the important thing."

"Only because Warren is gone," she huffs.

My ears prick. If he's gone, that means Chopper is outside. "How long ago did Warren leave?"

She shrugs. "A couple of minutes."

I dash to the front window and look outside. Warren and Chopper are talking. When that conversation ends, I need to be on Chopper's bike. "Beth, I need a dress for Matt's birthday dinner tonight. Can you bring something to the Grille later?"

She smiles, forgetting about her Warren drama in favor of getting to dress me up, something she weirdly loves to do. "I have the *perfect* outfit."

$$\sim 48 \sim$$

Today has been an almost normal day. Chopper brought me to the bar without a word being exchanged and I haven't seen hide nor hair of Warren. I even managed to get some accounting work done and sweet-talked Randy into calling Gary for me. They are restricting his calls, which makes sense because he's locked up and not supposed to have a phone, but it annoys me that I can't call him myself. The number is always blocked on their phones and I've noticed that even Warren has been switching his cell, jumping from burner to burner.

Warren *was* the first one who let me speak to Gary, though even when he's being decent, Warren is still Warren. The same as Beth will always be Beth. Her current fashion kick is all-things-red, but this time it isn't the shoes, it's the dress. If I had a chest like hers, I'd be X-rated in this skintight crimson mini that's cut so low, my bellybutton is practically hanging out. "You do know I'm going to dinner, right? Not on stage to work a pole."

"Exactly." She grins, putting the finishing touches on my hair. "Men are visual eaters. Might as well let Matt *see* his buffet."

My stomach cramps, trigging a pain in my side. I clutch at it. She frowns. "Are you sick?"

I shift in the chair where I'm sitting at Gary's table while she fusses with my locks. "No, I've just been having this weird pain. It starts in my back and then aches along my side, like I fell and got a deep bruise. But I don't remember falling."

"Probably why you're not allowed to drink anymore."

I swat her with the hairbrush. "I've only blacked out a couple of times."

"Five." She laughs. "Lately."

"Yeah, well, *lately* I've needed to drink." I rub my neck, a crick the size of Texas having formed. Probably because of the stress of having talked to Gary about me compiling notes from the guys while leaving out the part where *Matt* would be the one helping to set up the computer programming.

"All done!" Beth announces.

I clamber to my feet, walking as smoothly as I can in these skinny black heels. They're nothing more than spiked soles, fixed to me with black satin straps that Beth wrapped all the way up my legs, tying them into a bow that sits on the back of my thigh, just under the hem of my *very* short dress. I don't see the point of these so-called shoes but she said they're hot, and the mirror agrees with her, though I'm still not sure if I'm dressed to take my man to dinner or work a pole.

At any rate, I don't have a gift for Matt so the wrapping will have to do. Next year I'll blow him away with something good, like a new house with our names on the mailbox. "You really should go to cosmetology school, Beth. You made me look…completely different."

She laughs. "You're naturally beautiful. All I had to do was highlight what you're already working with. My sister, the beauty queen."

"Hardly." I think of the pageants I entered. They were all stupid. I wasn't there to win, only to appease Mom, who thought that was how I'd *hit it big* and drag us all out of this hole. I never really wanted to leave this town, though. All I ever wanted was just to be free in it. Funny how the ones who gave me that freedom are now the ones taking it away. "Matt's going to be here soon. Help me downstairs so I don't break my neck on the steps."

I'm well aware of what a half-naked woman does to a room full of men, and the fact that *I'm* the spectacle walking through the Grille has sweat building along my brow and a temper boiling under my surface. The Leidolf definitely look at women, but they don't catcall and act like morons. They have better sense and generally have respect for women. But this is me, so they're hamming it up, beating on tables, whistling and yelling. Bear and Freddie are even standing on their stools howling. With these stupid heels on I can't move fast enough to knock their legs out from under them.

Beth is beside me, shaking. I keep a course trained on the door and get her outside. "Bye." She breaks for her car.

"Hey!" I yell but she's already in her car and leaving me standing here alone. I turn my head left. Chopper is on his bike and Warren is standing next to him, the two of them frozen in place. "What? Never seen cleavage before?" I look away, watching down the street for Matt's car. He's been out of his office again today so now I have to stand here being a spectacle until he shows up.

"What will five dollars get me?" Dillon asks with a grin.

"Your throat ripped out."

He nods and walks on by me, entering the bar where the guys are still laughing. Matt's sedan pops around the corner and I do my best version of walking, heading out into the street to get in his passenger seat. He slams on his brakes, getting out of the car with a low whistle. "Holy…wow."

"You like?" I grin, giving him a flirty wink.

He runs around to open my door. "I *love*."

When Matt drops back into his driver's seat, Warren slides in the back. Matt looks at me. "Seriously?"

I shrug. "Just pretend he doesn't exist. That's what I do."

Matt's knuckles turn white on the wheel but he puts the car in gear and drives. I enter an address into his GPS and rest my hand on his knee. "I hope you're hungry."

His fingers trace along the satin thread wrapped around my thigh. "I'm starving."

"Pretending doesn't mean I *don't* exist," Warren pipes up, his phone flashing.

I turn to stare at him. He shrugs. "We just passed a gentleman's club. They're hiring."

I turn around. My phone vibrates and I glance at the screen. It's the picture Warren just took of the sign. I flip the visor down, pretending to check my makeup in the mirror but glaring at him instead. He smiles. I shove the visor back up and check the GPS. "Ten more minutes, Matt. Then we get rid of the shadow."

~49~

Warren

Tessa's house is quiet. Mostly. From my perch in the thick row of rhododendrons bordering her backyard, I hear the occasional moan. Groan. Noises that sound more animalistic than human. She was never like that with me. Loud. Vulgar. We were good together, though. *Very* good. So good that it was two years before I could even kiss another girl. I'd try, but their lips were all wrong. They didn't feel like her. Taste like her. They still don't, not even someone like Marcie, who makes me stand up and pay attention when she's around. I like her a lot. Marcie is sweet, pretty, and her temperament makes for a stress-free relationship. She's easy to please and pleases me easily. But she's not Tessa. Marcie doesn't feel quite right against my lips or wholly fit in my arms the way Tessa did. But my girl moved on from me a long time ago, so I'm *trying* to do the same.

Scrolling through my phone, I click on the photo Marcie and I took on the last date we had before the meeting in the bar, after which she promptly broke up with me. I've tried to get her back and we've talked some, but then I did the Rene thing, *for* Tessa even though Tessa won't even consider the possibility that I'd do anything at all for her. Which is crap, since I've been doing for Tessa my whole life.

I used to do anything I could to make her mad so she'd try getting even, then that boy grew into a teenager who'd do anything to make her smile. On my way to becoming a man, I

212

screwed up, and now I'm stuck trying to convince Marcie that being embedded at the Grille doesn't have anything to do with me still having feelings for Tessa.

I click the phone off, killing the light before I give away my location. I stare at the soft glow of light coming from Tessa's bedroom window. Occasionally I see shadows and look away. It's hard enough to be near her every day and outright brutal when I have to watch another man touch her. I may not mean anything to her, but Tessa is still a part of me. I feel her on me after all these years and can still pick up her scent in a crowd. She used to hide from me in the woods, laughing when I'd track her down and chase her through streams and over rocks. There was never a time when I couldn't find her. There have only been times when I couldn't have her.

Me still loving Tessa is why I can't convince Marcie otherwise. But if I could stop loving Tessa, I would have done it already. My phone vibrates and I unclench my teeth, hoping it's Gary telling me I'm released. That he's put the nail in Montrose and his plans to steer the club into human trafficking. Ever since I went to that auction in Ohio last year and heard tales of the Leidolf being involved in a sex ring in that area, I've been working with Gary to find out the truth of exactly *who* is involved. Because whoever it is doesn't only need to face justice, they need to stay away from Tessa.

"Yeah," I answer quietly.

"There's another body." Chopper's raspy voice makes me sit up straight.

"Who?"

"Woman by the name of Stella Ray. You know her?"

My jaw ticks. "Sort of. Marcie took me to meet her once. She's an estranged aunt, not much older than Marcie, though. And she doesn't live around here because she doesn't get along with Marcie's mom. Where was her body found?"

"In the river south of here. Kayakers found her. Chief told Gary she's been in the water a few days."

Bile rises in the back of my throat. This means there *has* been at least one murder since the curfew went into place, and it also means the killer isn't dropping every body where it can be easily found. There could be others. "I need to go to Marcie. Can you get here and watch Tessa?" I glance toward the window. "I think they're asleep now."

"Head on out. I'm already on my way."

~Tessa~

Chopper put me on the phone with Gary this morning. I should have known it was bad news when I found Chopper sitting on my couch, but my body is sore this morning, the pain I had yesterday was dull compared to what's happening in my back today. And of course, I can't remember most of what happened after Matt and I got home. We poured some shots to celebrate his birthday and I didn't think I drank that much, but the night is all darkness. I don't even have flashes of what we did. Something I can't tell Chopper, which means I can't tell him about the pain either.

I feel bad for being glad that I don't know the woman who was found dead. It's one less connection to me, and one more chink in the theory that the murders have something to do with me. Outside of that, another woman was murdered. That's all the motivation I need to forget about Matt being an ex-cop. I already have Gary's blessing so as soon as I get to my office, I start hashing out the plan for approaching the interviews with the guys.

Being trained in interrogation, Matt helps with the questions I should ask that would possibly spark a memory or draw out more details from the tight-lipped Leidolf. I even set up a speakerphone in my office so he could listen in and text me real-time changes to my script. He called Beth and had her come to his office to help him take notes so, between the three of us, we wouldn't miss anything.

~

What I'm doing with Matt and Beth is shady, but after three days and a dozen interviews, Matt's starting to see some connections. I'm just not sure they're helpful. For one, all of the guys have interacted with Hudson. He seems to be everywhere. But he's only a kid and I don't think he could do the damage to a female that's reported to have been done to these women. Not while they're alive anyway, and Chief told me yesterday that the coroner says the women aren't being sedated, they're being overpowered. As annoyed as I am with him and Gary both for their lackadaisical attitude about Gary being locked up, I mentioned Hudson to Chief and he agreed with me that it's improbable our killer is a bored teen who drives all over town hoping to be seen and find something to do.

Chopper picks up my arm, moving my shirt from where it got stuck on the back of my desk chair. "What's this?"

"I bumped into the stove," I lie, trying to think of something that would account for the bruise sitting just above my hip bone. It isn't like the bruise he gave me. This one is big and deep. His eyes narrow and I sigh. "I swear I'm not drinking. Much. Just a little bit to help me sleep."

He stares at me. I hand him my phone. "Ask Matt. He mixes me up one, maybe two cocktails. Delicious ones, by the way, we should have him show our bartenders, and—"

"Get ready for the funeral. You ride there with him, you come back with me."

"Hard to ride a motorcycle with a skirt on."

"Wear pants."

He slams my office door and I know not to push him. He's been tense since Warren left. We'll see Warren today, though.

He'll be with Marcie at Stella Ray's funeral, and after the club pays their respects, I hope to never have to see Warren again. Even with Chopper's tension, the last three days have been proof that we don't need Warren.

I didn't know Stella, and I can't say I care much for Marcie, especially after the lie she told about me supposedly saying something to her the day the curfew went into effect. I asked Beth if she'd heard anything and she admitted that *she'd* talked to Marcie, but said it was only in passing on account of them both running for their lives because of the *biker riot*. I'm not stupid, I know that information means Beth said something nippy to Marcie and Marcie blamed it on me, on the grounds of thinking I care enough about her to have an opinion on her relationship with Warren. But the fact that she repeated it to Warren as if *I'd* been the one to actually say whatever the words were, that crosses a line I won't easily forgive her for crossing.

Today, I'll quietly pay my respects, though. This killer has touched both our families and I want to stand with the others who are hurting the way we are. After the killer is behind bars, or more hopefully dead at the hands of vigilante justice, there will be time to finish what Marcie started.

Matt and I sit in the back of the church with nine Leidolf. Nine others, including Chopper, are outside. With Warren gone, I've been paying attention to who Chopper leaves me with and who he doesn't, trying to figure out which members he's skeptical of. He doesn't seem to have issues with anyone from our charter, but it's hard to tell because when Chopper isn't around, there's always a group of descendants, not just one or two.

Ahead of us in the front row, Warren cradled a sobbing Marcie until the service ended and her family formed a line near the closed casket, a beautiful picture of Stella encased in roses sitting atop the silver box. Row by row, we took our turns, staring into the eyes of a woman taken from this earth far too soon. Then we went down the line of family, expressing our condolences.

"I'm so sorry for your loss, Marcie." I offer the words and she reaches for me, drawing me into a hug, her tears hot on my shoulder. I glance at Warren. His hand is on her back, mouth drawn downward as he traces consoling circles against the fabric of her dress. I hold her, let her get out whatever she needs to expel because if there's anything I've learned, it's that grief is the oddest emotion of all. It drives us to places we never thought we'd go.

She lets go of me, sniffing. "I appreciate you coming. It means a lot."

"Of course." I wipe a tear from her cheek. "If you need anything, the club will take care of it. Just tell Warren. He'll let us know."

She looks up at him and smiles. "He's been a godsend. I don't know what I'd do without him."

Before I forget my manners, Matt's hand thrusts forward, a peace offering to Warren. I'm not surprised. Matt's the bigger man, literally and figuratively, and he's also the better man. "In times like these, we have to put aside our petty differences and support one another. I'm here for you, brother. Whatever you need, I'm here."

Tentatively, Warren accepts the handshake. "I appreciate it."

We walk away and I slide my hand into Matt's. "Thanks for trying to call a truce."

He nods. "If he stays away from you, it'll stay intact."

~

I wish I knew how to call a truce with Chopper. He didn't speak to me after we returned from the funeral other than telling me to stay in his apartment. I did, falling asleep on his bed, only to toss and turn in pain while he slept solidly on the couch. At some point, exhaustion took me, and now he's already waking me up. "We've got to go."

I rub my eyes. "Where?"

He swallows. "To Warren. Marcie's sister is dead."

I spring upright. "What? How? Which one?"

He presses his palms to my face. "They just found the youngest one dead. Warren needs us to come. He wants you to help with Marcie and her mom. Can you do that?"

I throw the sheets off me and get out of bed, ignoring the way my back feels broken. "I'll do anything I can but...what happened? Her sister is fourteen."

Chopper stares at me. My heart races. "*How* did she die, Chopper?"

"Her throat was cut."

~

Speculation stirs as I sit in Warren's house. It isn't finished yet, most of the walls still have exposed insulation. He built it in a section of woods behind the garage, surrounded by enough pine that the sounds of the garage and the road beyond are silenced. I had no idea he even had a house, let alone was building one as big as this.

Only two rooms are completed: the master bedroom with an en suite bathroom and the kitchen. We'd first occupied the bedroom but the smell of him overwhelmed me. He never wore cologne, and I could smell that he still doesn't. His odor is musky, deep earth with a hint of how the river smells on a crisp fall morning. I used to bury my face in his shirts at night, until the smell of him faded away with the passing days, just like my love for him.

Convincing Marcie that the air was better out in what will become the living room, I placed a plank of wood atop two buckets and we've been sitting here ever since. She's next to me, sobbing, which is better than how hysterical she was when Chopper and I arrived at her house. The police and ambulances were already there, swarming the driveway. Technically, Marcie lives on her mom's land, in a trailer parked just off the side of the driveway. In that driveway there were two cars and one motorcycle. The bike being Warren's, and one each of the cars belonging to Marcie and her mom. Teresa was found in her mom's car, sprawled across the backseat with her head nearly severed.

Warren is shaken, and he saw me look at his side where his knife had once been. "Bedroom." He'd nodded toward Marcie's place, telling me to go check his knife. I did. It was clean. I also checked the sinks. I'm not a forensic expert but there didn't appear to be any blood residue or paraphernalia one would use to clean up such a thing.

As soon as we could, we packed up Marcie and her mom and brought them here, getting them away from the scene while the police finish processing it. Marcie sniffs. "Chief said it might be a copycat killer. That things like this happen when murders get sensationalized. And you've seen the TV crews. They're everywhere now."

I can't avoid seeing them. They're stacked on top of each other across the street from the bar. Once in a while, a brave new face strolls into the bar, thinking they'll catch the club doing something nefarious while they eat a basket of fries. They usually leave in tears.

Marcie's mom paces in front of me, not hiding her disdain. "Someone killed my little girl to clear the *real* killer. Making us think he isn't *already* locked up."

Her daughter just died so I let accusation slide. Marcie doesn't, though. "There have been too many murders to still think it's Gary, Mom. I told you that already."

Her mom's nose lifts. "All I know is the same person who killed that tramp sister of mine didn't get ahold of my little Teresa. My daughter didn't associate with people like her." Her eyes hit on me, as if she's also lumping me in with the *likes* of Stella.

"She wasn't a tramp, Mom!" Marcie yells. "*Dad* had the affair, too! It wasn't just Stella all by herself!"

I'd heard their marriage ended over an affair, Marcie's mom never really kept quiet when she had an opportunity to bash her ex. I'd also heard some speculation that the affair was with the sister but that information came from *my* sister so I never took it as gospel.

Warren strolls into the room, kneeling down in front of Marcie and cupping her hands in his, talking softly to her. I can't help seeing the irony in Marcie's dad *and* her boyfriend both sleeping with their beloved's sister.

I sit beside them awkwardly until Warren stands, pulling the woman—who, it appears, will become his mother-in-law soon—into his arms. She clings to him and he holds her tight, corded muscles pulled taut as he whispers just as softly to her as he had to Marcie while the woman's grief comes out in torrents of tears and anger. "She would have fought. My Teresa wouldn't just lie there like that, she would have fought!"

Quietly, I get up and leave the house. I didn't know Teresa well. Mostly only saw her around town now and again, but she always reminded me of myself. She had no inhibitions and seemed to be friends with everyone and no one all at the same time. At her age, if someone put their hands on me, I would have fought hard enough to make them have to kill me. I'd do the same today. Same as I imagine Samantha would have. It makes me wonder if that's what happened to all of them. They fought, and their attacker liked it.

Walking up the gravel drive to where Chopper is parked in the turn just beyond the pines, I kneel down beside him. "What do you think? It isn't the same M.O., but it could still be the same person. Or are we really dealing with a copycat?"

He drops his cigarette butt to the ground. He normally doesn't smoke but this situation is getting the best of all of us and Chopper can't get blackout drunk every night the way I have been. "Warren thinks it's the same person."

"Why?"

He shrugs. "Something he saw in the body. He can't place his finger on what it is, but there was something."

I look back at the house. "Do you trust him?" Chopper's brow cocks. I swallow. "I'm not saying he's a murderer, I just…something is off about this whole thing. I don't believe the victims are random anymore, they do feel targeted. But Warren's giving us reasons that don't make any sense and these last two murders are only connected to him, as far as the club and I are concerned anyway."

Chopper stares at the cigarette beside his boot. "Warren thinks this last murder is a message."

"What kind of message does nearly decapitating a fourteen-year-old girl send?"

His eyes lift, shooting ice into my veins. "The killer is telling us he can walk right under our noses, and get to you."

~51~

Matt

Butterflies erupt as I pull into Tessa's driveway. She stayed at the bar last night and I missed her. Since that very first night with her, my desires about what I want for our future have been changing. Evolving. She's more special than I thought, and her house is one of the few places where I feel satisfied. Like I've been well-fed after a lifetime of starving.

She texted me an hour ago asking me to meet her at home. I expected a bike to be waiting outside but there isn't one. She's either not here yet, or she convinced the club to leave her alone for once.

Beth's car is here, so she's definitely home. I walk up the driveway, skimming my fingers along the hood of her car as my shoes crunch over the gravel and then sink into the soft earth where a sidewalk ought to be. Occasionally I step onto a chunk of long-forgotten concrete that's covered over by layers of soil and weeds, something I plan on fixing. I'll do it for Tessa *and* Beth, give them both a nice home to live in until we sell this one and buy something better.

"It's me," I announce as I open the door, tugging my shoes off and plopping them on the rubber mat where a pair of tennis shoes appear to have been kicked off in a hurry. Tessa doesn't wear tennis shoes. She hardly wears anything other than boots, so these are Beth's. My heart sinks. Tessa really might not be here yet.

"Babe?" I walk through the quiet house.

"In here!" Beth calls out from the direction of the bedrooms, hers just a stone's throw from Tessa's. I head down the hall, catching the flicker of light from Tessa's darkened room. I lightly push the ajar door open. My eyes adjust to the candlelight, bringing a vision of red into view. Beth is bent over the side table, her backside draped in what I vividly recall being my birthday gift. My throat tightens. "What are you doing wearing Tessa's dress?"

She lights her last candle and blows out the match, lifting herself upright and glancing at me over her shoulder. "Don't you like it?" She runs her hands along her thighs. "I picked this dress out just for you."

My palms sweat, mouth going dry as she spins toward me, her fingers grazing along the cleavage spilling out of the skimpy fabric. Unlike Tessa, Beth fills this dress out in a way that would have her arrested if she walked outside. "Where's Tessa? She asked me to meet her here."

She laughs, sitting on the bed and running her hand across the sheets. "That was me, silly. It's amazing what an app can do these days. I can text as her. Track her movements through the day even though the club gives her stupid burner phones." She points a manicured nail at me. "I even know when she's screwing you."

I run a hand through my hair. "Where is she right now?"

She smiles. "Wouldn't you like to know?"

"Yeah, Beth. I *would* like to know."

Her bright red lips blow me a kiss. "Don't worry, I'm keeping her busy."

I look around the room. There are candles lit on the dresser as well as both nightstands. "You've got her out chasing her tail so you can what? Pretend to be her?"

She slides farther back on the bed, positioning herself on all fours and crawling toward me. "Is that what you want, Matt? For me to pretend to be her?"

I move toward her. "No, Beth. I want you to be you, and Tessa to be Tessa. I didn't get to see her last night and now I'm finding out I haven't heard from her all day. *You've* been the one texting me." My gut burns. I bet she's done this a lot and the whole time I thought I was talking to Tessa. "*Where* is your sister?"

She sits back on her heels, legs parted. She doesn't have anything on under that dress. "What's the matter? Don't you like what you're seeing?"

I clear my throat, heart pounding. "You know I do."

She smiles. "Good. Because I've been getting worried that you prefer your women stupid."

"Tessa isn't stupid."

She slides the straps off her shoulders, letting her chest fill my eyes. "Isn't she? She can't even see what's right in front of her. Me. You. *Us.*" The bed creaks under her weight. "Your birthday night was especially fun. What you did to her, what *we* did to her." She licks her lips. "Don't worry. I'm not done with her yet. I like watching you with her. The way she's too stupid to know she's been drugged, and too stupid to know why her *poor little back* hurts the next day." She laughs, beckoning me forward. "I *love* how you hurt her, and I *love* when you take me right beside her. On top of her." She latches onto my hips and jerks me toward her. "All the things we do to her, I want you to do it all to me, right now."

My pulse beats in my ears, heart hammering against my chest. I remember the first time Beth bounced those breasts on top of me. We were in the back of my car, and made our first kill three days later. The very next day she promised me her sister. The plan was to torment Tessa, toy with her, take away all that was good in her life. But I don't want that anymore. I want more of what I've been having. Both of them. Only, I want to wean Tessa off the pills. I want her to feel what I do to her, and I want her to like it as much as Beth does.

I wrap my hand around Beth's throat. Her chest heaves, eyes dilating. I squeeze harder. Her back arches, her mouth parting in a groan. She has the same look on her face every time she wields her knife. Every time she brings it down on whoever I'm inside, driving me to climax. I flex my fingers, taunting her. "I've got a new plan."

Her nails dig into my forearms. "So do I." Her body presses forward, urging me to squeeze even harder. "I made a kill on my own last night. Punish me for it."

A Note From The Author

"Living the dream is simply a form of living your passion."
~ Urijah Faber

Thank you for reading *Descend!* This book has been rattling around in my head for years, the ending, anyway. It just took me a while to have the rest of the story fall into place and I hope you agree that it was well worth the wait because that ending is…everything.

While the characters and location of this book are complete fiction, I did take inspiration from a town close to where I grew up. Hinton is a great little riverside town so if you find yourself in southern West Virginia, look it up and take a country drive!

It's a fact that without my editor, everything I write would be complete rubbish. Anita from Proof Positive steered me in the right direction once again, and I can't thank her enough for her time and expertise. If there are mistakes in my manuscript, you better believe they're all mine.

To all the family, friends, and readers who continually support and encourage me, *thank you!* Dreaming is easy, it's daring to live a dream that's hard. You give me the confidence to continue and I'm eternally grateful. An extra dose of gratitude goes to my handsome husband Joe.

For my sailor, my hero, my son – thank you for unconditionally loving me. You are everything to me.

ABOUT THE AUTHOR

Lee Dawna is a thriller, suspense, and romance author living in the rolling mountains of West Virginia. An avid traveler and outdoorswoman, you may bump into her along a remote trail where a meandering stream whispers her next story.

Connect with her on:

Instagram https://www.instagram.com/leedawna_author/

Twitter https://twitter.com/LeeDawna_Author,

Facebook https://www.facebook.com/leedawnabooks

Find all her links in one place at
https://www.linktr.ee/LeeDawna

Book 3 of the romantic suspense Beller Ties set releases March 1st, 2022. Join my newsletter for early release news! https://mailchi.mp/c9aefdb4dab7/leedawna-books

Check out my website for direct-from-author special deals! https://leedawnabooks.com